PENGUIN BOOKS

# Maigret and the Idle Burglar

Georges Joseph Christian Simenon was born on 12 February 1903 in Liège, Belgium. He began work as a reporter for a local newspaper at the age of sixteen, and at nineteen he moved to Paris to embark on a career as a novelist. He started by writing pulp-fiction novels and novellas published, under various pseudonyms, from 1923 onwards. He went on to write seventy-five Maigret novels and twenty-eight Maigret short stories. Although Simenon is best known in Britain as the writer of the Maigret books, his prolific output of over 400 novels made him a household name and institution in Continental Europe, where much of his work is constantly in print. The dark realism of Simenon's books has lent them naturally to screen adaptation. Simenon died in 1989 in Lausanne, Switzerland, where he had lived for the latter part of his life.

# GEORGES SIMENON

# *Maigret and the Idle Burglar*

Translated by Daphne Woodward

PENGUIN BOOKS

PENGUIN BOOKS

Published by the Penguin Group
Penguin Books Ltd, 80 Strand, London WC2R ORL, England
Penguin Group (USA) Inc., 375 Hudson Street, New York, New York 10014, USA
Penguin Group (Canada), 90 Eglinton Avenue East, Suite 700,
Toronto, Ontario, Canada M4P 2Y3
(a division of Pearson Penguin Canada Inc.)
Penguin Ireland, 25 St Stephen's Green, Dublin 2, Ireland
(a division of Penguin Books Ltd)
Penguin Group (Australia), 250 Camberwell Road, Camberwell, Victoria 3124,
Australia (a division of Pearson Australia Group Pty Ltd)
Penguin Books India Pvt Ltd, 11 Community Centre,
Panchsheel Park, New Delhi – 110 017, India
Penguin Group (NZ), cnr Airborne and Rosedale Roads, Albany,
Auckland 1310, New Zealand (a division of Pearson New Zealand Ltd)
Penguin Books (South Africa) (Pty) Ltd, 24 Sturdee Avenue,
Rosebank, Johannesburg 2196, South Africa

Penguin Books Ltd, Registered Offices: 80 Strand, London WC2R ORL, England

www.penguin.com

First published as *Maigret et le voleur paresseux* 1961
This translation first published as *Maigret and the Lazy Burglar* by Hamish Hamilton 1963
Reissued, under the present title, with minor revisions, in Penguin Classics 2004
Published as a Penguin Red Classic 2006

I

Copyright © Georges Simenon Ltd, 1961
Translation copyright © Hamish Hamilton, 1963

All rights reserved

The moral right of the translator has been asserted

Set in 9.75/13.25 pt Trump Mediaeval
Typeset by Rowland Phototypesetting Ltd, Bury St Edmunds, Suffolk
Printed in England by Clays Ltd, St Ives plc

ISBN-13: 978-0-141-02962-7
ISBN-10: 0-141-02962-5

# Chapter One

A shrill noise broke out close to Maigret's ear, and he stirred crossly, as though startled, flapping one arm outside the bed-clothes. He was aware of being in bed, and aware of his wife's presence at his side, wider awake than himself, lying in the dark without venturing to speak.

Where he was mistaken – at least for a few seconds – was about the nature of the insistent, aggressive, imperious sound. And it was always in winter, in very cold weather, that he made this mistake.

He thought his alarm clock was ringing, although never since his marriage had there been one at his bedside. The idea went back even further than his boyhood – to the time when, as a small choirboy, he used to serve at mass at six o'clock in the morning.

Yet he had served at mass in spring, summer and autumn as well. Why did this one memory persist, returning to him unbidden – a memory of darkness, frost, stiff fingers, and thin ice in the lane, crackling underfoot?

He upset his glass of water, as often happened, and Madame Maigret switched on the bedside lamp just as his fumbling hand reached the telephone.

'Maigret here . . . Yes . . .'

It was ten minutes past four, and the silence outside was the special silence of the coldest winter nights.

'This is Fumel, superintendent . . .'

'What d'you say?'

He could scarcely hear. It sounded as if the caller had a handkerchief stuffed in his mouth.

'Fumel, of the 16th . . .'

The man spoke softly, as though afraid of being overheard by someone in the next room. When the superintendent made no response, he added:

'Aristide . . .'

Oh – Aristide Fumel! Maigret was wide awake now, and wondering why the devil Inspector Fumel, of the 16th *arrondissement*, had woken him at four in the morning.

And also why he was speaking in that mysterious, almost furtive voice.

'I don't know if I'm right to telephone you . . . I informed my immediate superior, the superintendent at my own station, right away. He told me to ring the public prosecutor's office and I spoke to the official on night duty there . . .'

Although Madame Maigret could hear nothing except her husband's replies, she was already out of bed, her toes groping for her bedroom slippers. She wrapped her quilted dressing-gown round her and went off to the kitchen, whence came the hissing sound of gas and then the splash of water as she filled the kettle.

'One never knows what to do nowadays, if you see what I mean. The public prosecutor's assistant told me to go back to the spot and wait for him. I didn't find the body myself, it was two of the cycle-patrol chaps . . .'

'Where?'

'Beg pardon?'

'I asked where?'

'In the Bois de Boulogne . . . Route des Poteaux . . . You know it? It's a turning off the Avenue Fortunée, not far from the Porte Dauphine . . . A middle-aged man . . . About my age . . . So far as I could make out, his pockets were empty, no identity papers . . . I didn't move the body, of course . . . I can't say why, but it strikes me there's something queer about it, and I felt I'd like to ring you . . . It would be as well for the Public Prosecutor's people not to know . . .'

'Thanks, Fumel . . .'

'I'll be getting back there at once, in case they turn up quicker than usual.'

'Where are you now?'

'In the station in the Rue de la Fraisanderie. Will you be coming along?'

Maigret, snug in his warm bed hesitated, then said:

'Yes.'

'What'll you say?'

'Don't know yet. I'll think of something.'

He was feeling humiliated, almost angry, not for the first time in the past six months. Fumel was a good chap, it wasn't his fault.

Madame Maigret appeared in the doorway to advise:

'Dress up warmly. It's freezing hard.'

Drawing back the curtain, he saw frost-flowers on the window. The street lamps had the special brightness that only comes with intense cold, and along the Boulevard Richard-Lenoir there was not a soul to be seen or a sound to be heard – just one lighted window, in the house opposite; must be someone ill there.

So now 'they' were forcing the police to play tricks! By 'they' he meant the public prosecutor's department, the crowd at the Ministry of the Interior – the whole bunch of college-educated law-givers who had taken it into their heads to run the world according to their own little ideas.

They looked on the police force as a minor, slightly discreditable cog in the wheel of Justice with a capital J – one to regard with suspicion, to watch out for, to keep in its place.

Like Janvier, Lucas and a score or so of Maigret's men, Fumel was the old-fashioned kind; but the others had adjusted themselves to the new methods and rules – all they thought of was passing exams so as to get quicker promotion.

Poor Fumel had stuck at the bottom of the ladder because he could never learn to spell or to draw up a report!

Nowadays the public prosecutor insisted that he or one of his staff should be the first to be informed and the first on the scene, accompanied by a sleepy examining magistrate; and the pair of them would give their views as though they'd spent their entire lives finding corpses and knew more about criminals than anyone else.

As for the police, they were sent on errands . . . 'You're to do such and such . . . You're to arrest so-and-so and bring him to my office . . .

'And mind you don't ask him any questions! We must keep strictly to the regulations.'

There were so many regulations – the *Journal Officiel* published shoals, which sometimes contradicted one another – that even the magistrates lost their way among them and went in terror of being caught out by some protesting counsel.

Maigret dressed himself, crossly. Why did the coffee always taste different on winter nights when he was woken up like this? The flat had a different smell, too, one that reminded him of his parents' house in the days when he used to get up at half-past five every morning.

'Will you telephone to the office for a car?'

No! If he arrived on the scene in an official car, they might ask what he was up to.

'Ring for a taxi from the rank.'

He wouldn't get a refund, unless he caught the murderer very quickly – assuming it was a murder. Taxi fares were only refunded if you were successful, these days. And even then you had to prove that there had been no other way of getting to the spot.

His wife handed him a thick, woolly muffler.

'Have you got your gloves?'

He felt in his overcoat pocket.

'Won't you have something to eat?'

He was not hungry. His manner was glum, and yet at bottom this was the kind of moment he enjoyed – even, perhaps, what he would miss most after he retired.

He went downstairs and found a taxi at the door, white steam puffing out of its exhaust.

'The Bois de Boulogne . . . You know the Route des Poteaux?'

'It'd be a poor show if I didn't, after thirty-five years at this job.'

It was with that kind of talk that the older drivers consoled themselves for the passage of time.

The leather upholstery was ice-cold. They met only a few cars, and an occasional empty bus making for its terminus. Even the earliest bars were still in darkness. Cleaners were at work in the offices along the Champs-Élysées.

'Another tart got herself knocked off?'

'I don't know . . . I don't think so.'

'I was thinking she wouldn't find many clients in the Bois in weather like this.'

Maigret's pipe tasted different, too. He thrust his hands deeper into his pockets, reflecting that it must be at least three months since he last met Fumel and that he had known him since . . . almost ever since he himself had joined the force, when he'd been attached to one of the district police stations.

Fumel had been ugly even in those days, and even then the other men had pitied and laughed at him – partly because his parents had been misguided enough to christen him Aristide and partly because, in spite of his appearance, he was always involved in some love-drama.

He married, and after a year his wife disappeared. He moved heaven and earth to find her. For years, every policeman in

France had carried her description in his pocket, and Fumel used to rush to the morgue whenever a woman's body was fished out of the Seine.

The thing had become a byword.

'I can't get it out of my head that something dreadful has happened to her and that it was me they were aiming at,' he would say.

He had a wall-eye – immobile and paler than the other, almost transparent; it made you feel embarrassed when he looked at you.

'I shall love her all my life ... And I know I shall find her some day.'

Was he still clinging to that hope, now he'd reached fifty-one? It didn't prevent him from falling in love at intervals; and his bad luck persisted, for his affairs invariably landed him in incredible complications and ended disastrously.

He had even been accused of living on immoral earnings – this on the apparently convincing evidence of a strumpet who was making a fool of him – and had narrowly escaped being dismissed from the force.

How did a man so ingenuous and awkward in private life manage to be one of the best police inspectors in Paris?

The taxi entered the Bois by the Porte Dauphine and turned to the right. The glow of a pocket torch could already be seen ahead, and soon they came to where some shadowy figures stood beside a path.

Maigret got out and paid the taxi. One of the figures came up to him. It was Fumel.

'You've got here before them ...' breathed the inspector stamping on the frozen ground to warm his feet.

There were two bicycles propped against a tree. The cycle police, in their capes, were stamping about too, while a little man in a light-grey felt hat glanced impatiently at his watch.

Doctor Boisrond, from the registrar's department ...

Maigret shook the doctor's hand absent-mindedly and strolled over to a dark shape lying at the foot of a tree. Fumel turned his torch on it.

'I think you'll see what I mean, superintendent,' he began, 'It strikes me there's something fishy . . .'

'Who found him?'

'These two cycle-patrol men, going their round . . .'

'What time was it?'

'Twelve minutes past three. At first they thought it was a sack someone had dropped there.'

And indeed, the man lying in the stiff-frozen grass looked like a shapeless bundle. He was not stretched out, but huddled, almost curled up, except that one hand projected, the fingers still clenched as though trying to clutch at something.

'What did he die of?' Maigret asked the doctor.

'I was a bit frightened to touch him before the Public Prosecutor's men arrive, but so far as I can tell his skull was fractured by a blow, or blows, from some very heavy object . . .'

'His skull?' queried the superintendent.

For the light of the pocket torch showed him a bruised and blood-stained mass where the face should have been.

'I can't say for certain before the post-mortem, but I would almost swear those blows were struck afterwards, when the man was already dead, or at least dying . . .'

Whereupon Fumel peered at Maigret through the semi-darkness and said:

'You see what I mean, chief?'

The clothes on the body were good but not expensive – like those of a civil servant or a retired business executive.

'You say there's nothing in his pockets?'

'I felt them cautiously and there were no bulges . . . Now, take a look around . . .'

Fumel moved the beam of his torch over the ground near the man's head; there was no trace of blood.

'It wasn't here that he was coshed. The doctor agrees, because from the nature of the wounds he must have bled freely. So he was brought to the Bois – by car, no doubt. From the way he's huddled up, one would even say he was simply pushed out of the car – that the chaps who brought him didn't bother to get out themselves.'

The Bois de Boulogne lay silent, lifeless as an empty stage, its widely spaced lamps casting perfect circles of white light.

'Look out . . . Here they are, I think.'

A car was approaching from the direction of the Porte Dauphine – a long, black car, seeking its way. Fumel hurried to meet it, waving his torch.

Maigret stood back, puffing at his pipe.

'This is the place, sir . . . The superintendent had to go to the Hôpital Cochin for an identification; he'll be here in a few minutes.'

Maigret recognized the public prosecutor's deputy, a tall, thin, elegant man about thirty years old, whose name was Kernavel. He also recognized the examining magistrate, as it happened, though he had seldom worked with him: a certain Cajou, a dark-haired fellow in his early forties, who stood, as it were, midway between the old generation and the new. The clerk who accompanied them kept well away from the corpse, as though afraid the sight would turn his stomach.

'Who . . .' began the deputy prosecutor.

He looked at Maigret's shadowy figure and frowned.

'Excuse me. I didn't see you at first. How do you come to be here?'

Maigret replied with a vague gesture and the even vaguer words:

'By accident.'

Kernavel was annoyed; he went on speaking ostensibly to Fumel:

'What exactly happened?'

'Two cycle-patrol men were on their round when they noticed the body, just over an hour ago. I reported to my local superintendent, but as I explained, he had to go to the Hôpital Cochin for an urgent identification and he instructed me to inform your department. As soon as I had done so, I telephoned to Doctor Boisrond.'

The deputy prosecutor looked round for the doctor.

'What did you find, doctor?'

'A fracture of the skull; probably multiple fractures.'

'An accident? You don't suppose he was knocked down by a car?'

'He was struck several times with a blunt instrument, first on the head and then in the face.'

'So you're certain it was murder?'

Maigret could have held his tongue, left things to them, let them go on talking. But he took a step forward.

'It might save time, perhaps, if the Judicial Identity experts were informed.'

The prosecutor's man said, still addressing himself to Fumel:

'Send one of the cycle men to telephone.'

He was blue with cold. They were all cold, standing round the motionless body.

'A night prowler?'

'He's not dressed like a vagrant, and in this weather they don't come much to the Bois.'

'Been robbed?'

'For all I know – there's nothing in his pockets.'

'Attacked on his way home?'

'There's no blood on the ground. The doctor thinks – and so do I – that the crime was not committed here.'

'In that case it was most likely a private vendetta.'

The deputy prosecutor spoke emphatically, pleased at having found a satisfactory explanation of the problem.

'The crime was probably committed in Montmartre and the gang that did it got rid of the body by dumping it here . . .'

He turned to Maigret:

'I don't think this is a matter for you, superintendent. You no doubt have some important cases on hand. Oh, yes – where have you got to over that Post Office hold-up in the 13th *arrondissement*?'

'Nowhere, as yet.'

'And the previous hold-ups? How many have we had, in Paris alone, in the last fortnight?'

'Five.'

'That's the figure I seemed to remember. So I'm rather surprised to find you here, concerning yourself with a matter of no importance.'

It was not the first time Maigret had heard this kind of thing. The Public Prosecutor's people were alarmed by the crime wave, as they called it, and particularly by the sensational robberies which had been, for some time past, in one of their recurrent periods of crescendo.

It meant that a new gang had been formed recently.

'You still have no clues?'

'None whatsoever.'

This was not absolutely true. Though he had no actual evidence, Maigret had formed a theory that held together and seemed to be borne out by events. But that did not concern anyone else, least of all the public prosecutor's department.

'Listen, Cajou, you can handle this business. If you'll take my advice it will be least said, soonest mended. It's a commonplace incident, a quarrel in the underworld, and if the gangsters take to killing one another, so much the better for the rest of us. You see what I mean?'

He turned to Fumel again.

'You're an inspector in the 16th *arrondissement*?'

Fumel nodded.

'How long have you been in the force?'

'Thirty years . . . Twenty-nine, to be precise.'

'Has he a good record?' Kernavel asked Maigret.

'He's a man who knows his job.'

Kernavel took the examining magistrate aside and talked to him in an undertone. When the two of them came back, Cajou seemed rather embarrassed.

'Well, superintendent, thank you for coming along. I'll keep in touch with Inspector Fumel and give him my instructions. If a time comes when I think he needs help, I'll send someone to ask for your views, or get you to come to my office. Your own work is so important and so urgent that I must not delay you here any longer.'

It was not only from cold that Maigret's face had turned pale, and he bit so hard on the stem of his pipe that it made a faint cracking sound.

'Gentlemen . . .' he said, as though in farewell.

'Have you a car?' asked the deputy prosecutor.

'I shall find a taxi at the Porte Dauphine.'

Kernavel hesitated, on the point of offering to drive him there; but the superintendent was already walking away, after a little wave of the hand to Fumel.

And yet, half an hour later, Maigret would no doubt have been able to tell them a good deal about the dead man. He was not certain as yet, that was why he had said nothing.

The moment he bent to look at the body he felt this was someone he had seen before. Although the face had been battered to pulp, he could have sworn he recognized it.

All he needed was one scrap of evidence, and that would be found when the body was undressed.

If he was right, of course, the fingerprints would point to the same conclusion.

On the rank he found the taxi that had brought him.

'Finished already?'

'Take me home to the Boulevard Richard-Lenoir.'

'Okay. But talk about quick work . . . Who is it?'

A bar was open in the Place de la République, and Maigret was tempted to stop the taxi and go in for a glass of something. He refrained, however, feeling it would not be quite the thing.

His wife had gone back to bed, but she heard him on the stairs, and got up to open the door. She, too, was surprised:

'Back already?' she asked, adding at once, anxiously:

'What's happening?'

'Nothing. Those gentlemen didn't need me.'

He said as little as possible about it to her. He seldom mentioned the Quai des Orfèvres and its affairs in his own home.

'Have you had anything to eat?'

'No.'

'I'll get breakfast ready. You'd better have a bath right away, to warm you up.'

He did not feel cold. His anger had given way to depression.

He wasn't the only member of the Judicial Police who had a sense of discouragement, and the Director had twice threatened to resign. He would not have a third opportunity of doing so, because the question of his successor was already under consideration.

The place was being reorganized, as they called it. Well-educated, gentlemanly young fellows, scions of the best French families, were sitting in quiet offices, studying the whole thing in the interests of efficiency. Their learned cogitations were producing impractical plans that found expression in a weekly batch of new regulations. To begin with, the police were now declared to be an instrument at the service of justice. A mere instrument. And an instrument has no brain.

It was now the examining magistrate in his office and the Public Prosecutor in his awe-inspiring headquarters who directed investigations and gave orders.

What was more, the orders were no longer to be carried out by the old-fashioned type of policeman, the traditional 'flatties' such as Aristide Fumel, some of whom didn't know how to spell.

Now that it was nearly all paperwork, what was to be done with such men, who had learnt their job in the streets, the department stores and the railway stations, getting to know every drinking den in their own districts, acquainted with every tough and every tart, and able, if need be, to argue with them in their own language?

Now they had to sit for exams and obtain certificates at every step of their career, and when he needed to organize a raid, Maigret had nobody to rely on except the few survivors of his old team.

'They' were not pushing him out yet. They were biding their time, knowing he was only two years short of retirement age.

But they were beginning to keep a close eye on him.

It was still dark as he ate his breakfast, while the windows across the street lit up, one after another. Because of that telephone call he was earlier than usual, and a bit sluggish, as one is after too little sleep.

'Fumel – isn't that the one who squints?'

'Yes.'

'And whose wife ran away?'

'Yes.'

'Was she ever found?'

'It seems she's in South America, married again and with a swarm of children.'

'Does he know?'

'What would be the point?'

Maigret got to the office early, too, and though it was at last beginning to grow light, he was obliged to turn on his green-shaded lamp.

'Get me the all-night station in the Rue de la Faisanderie, please.'

It was he who was wrong. He didn't want to grow sentimental.

'Hello? Is Inspector Fumel there? What's that? Writing up his report?'

Always this paperwork, this form-filling, this waste of time.

'That you, Fumel?'

The other man was again speaking below his breath, as though making a surreptitious call.

'Have the Identity people finished their job?'

'Yes. They left an hour ago.'

'Did the official pathologist turn up?'

'Yes. The new one.'

For there was a new official pathologist as well. Old Doctor Paul, who had gone on making post-mortems till he was seventy-six, had died and been succeeded by a man called Lamalle.

'What does he say?'

'The same as the first doctor. The man wasn't killed where we found him. He must have bled a great deal, no doubt about that. The last blows, in the face, were struck after the chap was dead.'

'Did they undress him?'

'Partly.'

'You didn't notice a tattoo mark on the left arm?'

'How did you know?'

'A fish . . . A kind of sea-horse?'

'Yes . . .'

'Did they take his fingerprints?'

'By now they'll be dealing with them in Records.'

'The body's gone to the Medico-Legal Institute?'

'Yes . . . You know, I felt very uncomfortable just now . . . I still do . . . But I didn't like to . . .'

'You can put in your report that in all probability the victim is a certain Honoré Cuendet, a Swiss from Vaud, who at one time spent five years in the Foreign Legion.'

'The name rings a bell . . . Do you know where he lived?'

'No. But I know where his mother lives, if she's still alive. I'd rather be the first to talk to her.'

'*They* will find out.'

'I don't care. Make a note of the address, but don't go there before I give you the word. She lives in the Rue Mouffetard. I don't know the number, but it's just above a bakery, nearly at the corner of the Rue Saint-Médard.'

'Thank you, chief.'

'That's all right. Are you staying on in the office?'

'It'll take me a good two or three hours to write this blasted report.'

Maigret had been right, and it gave him a certain satisfaction, mingled with a touch of melancholy. Leaving his office, he climbed a flight of stairs to the records department, where men in grey overalls were busily at work.

'Who's dealing with the prints of the man found dead in the Bois de Boulogne?'

'I am, superintendent.'

'Traced him?'

'Just this moment.'

'Cuendet?'

'Yes.'

'Thanks.'

Feeling almost lively by this time, Maigret went along a succession of corridors till he came to the attics of the Palais de Justice. Here, among the Judicial Identity experts, he found his old friend Moers, who was also poring over some forms. Never had there been such a clutter of papers as in the last six months. It was true that even in the old days the administrative work had been considerable; but Maigret estimated that it had recently begun to take up about eighty per cent of the time of all police personnel.

'Have they brought you the clothes?'

'Of the chap in the Bois de Boulogne?'

'Yes.'

Moers pointed to two of his men, who were shaking big paper bags containing the dead man's clothes. This was routine procedure, the first technical operation. In this way all kinds of dust was collected and subsequently analysed, sometimes yielding valuable clues – for example, as to what had been the occupation of some unidentified man, or where he usually lived, or sometimes as to the place where the crime had actually been committed.

'Pockets?'

'Nothing. No watch, no pocket-book, no keys. Not even a handkerchief. Literally nothing.'

'Any laundry-marks, or tabs on his suit?'

'Yes, those weren't torn out or cut off. I made a note of the tailor's name. Do you want it?'

'Not at present. The man's been identified.'

'Who is he?'

'An old acquaintance of mine, a fellow called Cuendet.'

'A criminal?'

'A quiet man, probably the quietest burglar there ever was.'

'D'you think it was an accomplice who did the job?'

'Cuendet never had an accomplice.'

'Why was he killed?'

'That's just what I'm wondering.'

Here again they were working by artificial light, as in most Paris offices on that particular day. The sky was a steely grey, and out in the street the pavement looked as black as though it were coated with ice.

People were walking fast, keeping close to the houses, a little cloud of vapour floating in front of each mouth.

Maigret went back to his inspectors. Two or three of them were on the telephone, but the majority, inevitably, were writing.

'Any news, Lucas?'

'We're still hunting for old Fernand. Someone thinks he saw him in Paris three weeks ago, but can't say for certain.'

An old lag. Ten years ago this Fernand, whose identity had never been definitely established, was a member of a gang that had brought off an impressive number of hold-ups in the space of a few months.

The whole bunch had been arrested, and the case had dragged on for nearly two years. The leader had died in prison, of TB. A few of his subordinates were still behind bars, but the time had come when they were being released, one by one, as the result of good-conduct remissions.

Maigret had not mentioned this just now to the deputy public prosecutor, when he expressed such alarm about the 'new crime-wave'. He had his own ideas on the subject. Certain points about the recent hold-ups had led him to believe that some of the old crowd were mixed up in the business, had no doubt formed a new gang.

All that was needed was to find one of them. And every man who could be spared had been working patiently to that end for nearly three months.

Their inquiries had finally centred on Fernand. He had been released a year ago, and for the last six months there had been no sign of him.

'His wife?'

'She still swears she hasn't seen him. The neighbours bear her out. No one has seen Fernand in that district.'

'Carry on, boys . . . If anyone asks for me . . . If anyone from the public prosecutor's department asks for me . . .'

He paused, then added:

'Say I've gone out for a drink. Say whatever you like.'

All the same, they were not going to stop him dealing with a man he had known for thirty years and who was almost a personal friend.

# Chapter Two

It was rare for Maigret to talk about his work, and even rarer for him to pass judgement on any individual or method. He mistrusted ideas as being always too specific to fit the circumstances – which, he knew by experience, were in a state of perpetual flux.

Only to his friend Doctor Pardon, who lived in the Rue Popincourt, did he occasionally, after dinner, mutter something that might, at a pinch, be regarded as confidential.

It so happened that a few weeks before this he had gone to the point of declaring with some bitterness:

'You know, Pardon, people imagine we're there to track down criminals and get confessions from them. That's just another of the mistaken notions that drift around until everybody is so used to them that nobody thinks of calling them in question. In point of fact our chief job is to protect the State in the first place – whatever government is in power, with its institutions; in the second place the currency, public property and private property; and then, last of all, the lives of the individual citizens.

'Did you ever take a look into the Penal Code? You have to read as far as page 177 before you come to anything about crimes against human beings. One day later on, when I retire, I'll work it out precisely. But let's say that three-quarters of the Code, if not four-fifths, is concerned with goods and chattels, real estate, forged currency, forgeries of public and private documents, falsification of wills, etc., etc. In short, with money in all its shapes and forms . . . To such an extent that Article 274, on mendicancy, comes before Article 295, on wilful homicide . . .'

This although they had dined well that evening, and drunk an unforgettable Saint-Emilion.

'The newspapers give the greatest amount of space to my service – The Crime Squad, as it has come to be called – because it's the most sensational. But in actual fact we're less important, in the eyes of the Minister of the Interior, for example, than General Information or the Finance Section.

'We're rather like barristers in court. We make a show, but it's the back-room boys who do the serious work.'

Would he have talked like that twenty years ago? Or even six months ago, before the changes he was watching with so much misgiving?

He muttered to himself as, with his coat collar turned up, he crossed the Pont Saint-Michel, leaning against the north wind at the same angle as all the other pedestrians.

He often talked to himself like this, with a surly expression on his face; and one day he had overheard Lucas telling Janvier, then a newcomer to the Préfecture:

'Take no notice. When he's in a brown study it doesn't necessarily mean he's in a bad temper.'

Nor even that he was depressed. Only that something was nagging at him. Today it was the attitude of the public prosecutor's men in the Bois de Boulogne, and also the stupid end that Honoré Cuendet had come to, with his face battered to pulp after his skull had been smashed in.

*Tell 'em I've gone out for a drink.*

That's what things had come to. What interested the gentlemen in high places was to put a stop to the series of attacks that were causing losses to banks, insurance companies and the Post Office. They also considered that car-thefts were becoming too frequent.

'What about giving more protection to the cashiers?' he had expostulated. 'Why leave one man, or a couple of men, to convey millions of francs by a route that anyone can find out beforehand?'

Too expensive, of course.

As for the private cars, was it reasonable to leave such things – worth a fortune, in some cases the price of an average flat, or of a little house in the suburbs – parked along the kerb, sometimes without locking the doors or even removing the ignition key?

You might as well leave a diamond necklace, or a wallet containing two or three million francs, in a place where any Tom, Dick or Harry could pick it up.

And so what? It was none of his business. He, more than ever, was a mere instrument, and such questions didn't come within his range.

All the same, he went to the Rue Mouffetard where, despite the cold, he found the usual bustle going on round the pavement stalls and the hand-barrows. Two doors beyond the Rue Saint-Médard he recognized the narrow, yellow-painted front of the bakery, and above it the windows of the *entresol*.

The house was an old one, tall and narrow. From the far end of the courtyard came the noise of hammering on iron.

Maigret went up the stairs, where there was a rope by way of banisters, and knocked at a door. Soon he heard soft footsteps.

'Is that you, dear?' a voice inquired, as the handle turned and the door opened.

The old woman had grown even fatter, but only in her lower half, from the waist downwards. She had a thinnish face and narrow shoulders, but her hips had become enormous, so enormous that she could hardly walk.

She stared at Maigret in alarmed astonishment, with the expression to which he was accustomed in such people, who went in dread of some misfortune.

'I know you, don't I? You've been here before . . . Wait a minute . . .'

'Superintendent Maigret . . .' he muttered, stepping into a room that was full of warmth and the smell of stew.

'Yes, that's it . . . I remember . . . What have you got against him this time?'

She gave no impression of hostility, only of a kind of resignation, an acceptance of fate.

She pointed to a chair. There was only one armchair in the room, a shabby leather affair, and that was occupied by a small sandy-haired dog who bared his pointed teeth with a low growl, and a cat – white with coffee-coloured spots – who scarcely opened his green eyes.

'Quiet, Toto,' said the woman – adding to Maigret, 'He just growls, but he's not dangerous. He's my son's dog. I don't know whether it's from living with me, but he's grown to look like me.'

And indeed, the beast had a tiny head with a pointed nose, and spindly legs, but its body was plump, more like a pig's than a dog's It seemed very old. It had yellow teeth, with gaps between them.

'Honoré picked him up in the street, at least fifteen years ago; he'd had two legs broken by a car . . . Honoré put them into splints, though the neighbours wanted to have the dog put down; and two months later he was running about with the best of them.'

The room had a low ceiling and was rather dark, but remarkably clean. It served both as kitchen and dining-room; there was a round table in the middle, an old dresser, and a Dutch cooking-stove of a type seldom seen nowadays. Cuendet must have bought it in the flea-market or from a junk dealer, and refurbished it – he had always been clever with his hands. The iron top was nearly red-hot, the brass bits glittered, and it made a faint roaring sound.

Outside, the street market was in full swing and Maigret remembered that at his last visit he had found the old woman leaning out of the window; in fine weather she spent most of her time like that, watching the crowd below.

'Well, superintendent?'

She still spoke in the slow accents of her native Switzerland, and instead of sitting down opposite him she remained standing, on the defensive.

'When did you last see your son?'

'Tell me first whether you've arrested him yet.'

After only a second's hesitation he was able to answer, truthfully:

'No.'

'In other words, you're looking for him? In that case I can tell you at once that he isn't here. You can search the place, as you've done before. You'll find no changes, although that was over ten years ago.'

She pointed to an open door and he looked through into a dining-room that was never used; it was cluttered with useless ornaments, doilies and framed photographs – typical of humble people who are nevertheless determined to keep one room 'for best'.

The superintendent remembered that there were two bedrooms, overlooking the courtyard – the old woman's, which had an iron bedstead by which she set great store, and the one Honoré sometimes used, which was almost as plain but more comfortable.

The smell of fresh-baked bread rose from the ground floor and mingled with the smell of stew.

Maigret was grave, even a little moved.

'I'm not looking for him either, Madame Cuendet. I would just like to know . . .'

At once she seemed to understand, to guess, and she stared at him more keenly, a glint of anxiety in her eyes.

'If you're not looking for him and you haven't arrested him, it means that . . .'

She had thinning hair and the top of her head looked absurdly small.

'Something's happened to him, isn't that it?'

He bowed his head.

'I thought I'd rather tell you myself.'

'The police shot him?'

'No . . . I . . .'

'An accident?'

'Your son is dead, Madame Cuendet.'

She gazed at him fixedly, dry-eyed, and the sandy dog, which seemed to understand, jumped down from the armchair and came over to rub against her fat legs.

'Who did it?'

The words were forced out between teeth as widely spaced as those of the dog, which began growling again.

'I don't know. He was killed, but we don't yet know where.'

'Then how can you tell . . .'

'His body was found this morning beside one of the paths in the Bois de Boulogne.'

She repeated the words, mistrustfully, as thought still scenting a trap.

'In the Bois de Boulogne? What would he be doing in the Bois de Boulogne?'

'That's where he was found. He had been killed somewhere else and brought there by car.'

'Why?'

He was patient, careful not to rush her, taking his time.

'That's what we're wondering ourselves.'

How could he have explained his attitude towards Cuendet to the examining magistrate, for instance? It wasn't only in his office on the Quai des Orfèvres that he had come to know the man. And that first rather slapdash investigation had not been enough. It had taken thirty years of his professional life and several visits to this flat, where he no longer felt like a stranger.

'It's in order to find his murderers that I need to know when you saw him for the last time. He hadn't slept here for some days, had he?'

'At his age a man surely has the right . . .'

She broke off, her eyes suddenly filling with tears, and asked: 'Where is he now?'

'You'll see him presently. An inspector will come to fetch you.'

'He's been taken to the morgue?'

'To the Medico-Legal Institute – yes.'

'Did he suffer?'

'No.'

'They shot him?'

Tears were running down her cheeks, but she was not sobbing, and there was still a shade of distrust in her expression as she stared at Maigret.

'They coshed him.'

'What with?'

She seemed to be trying to reconstruct her son's death in her own mind.

'We don't know. Something heavy.'

Instinctively she raised a hand to her head, with a grimace of pain.

'Why?'

'We shall find out, I promise you. That is why I've come here and why I need your help. Sit down, Madame Cuendet.'

'I can't.'

But her knees were shaking.

'Haven't you anything to drink?'

'You're thirsty?'

'No. It's for you. I'd like you to take a nip of something.'

He remembered she was fond of her glass, and at this, sure enough, she went to the dining-room sideboard and brought out a bottle of plum brandy.

Even at such a moment she couldn't resist cheating a bit.

'I was keeping it for my son ... He sometimes took a drop after dinner.'

She filled two thick-bottomed glasses.

'I wonder why they killed him,' she resumed. 'A lad who never harmed a soul – the quietest, gentlest man in the world ... Wasn't he, Toto? You know that better than anyone ...'

As she wept, she patted the fat dog, who wagged his stump of a tail. The deputy prosecutor and Cajou, the examining magistrate, would no doubt have found the scene ludicrous.

After all, the son she was talking about was an ex-convict and would still have been in prison, but for his own cleverness.

He had only gone there twice, and on one occasion merely while awaiting trial. Both times it had been Maigret who had arrested him.

They had spent hours and hours in solitary conversation at the Quai des Orfèvres, fencing with one another as though each appreciated the other at his full value.

'How long is it since ...'

Maigret returned to the attack, patiently, speaking in level tones against a background of market noises.

'A good month,' she said, giving way at last.

'He didn't tell you anything?'

'He never told me about anything he did outside this house.'

That was true, as Maigret had discovered in the old days.

'He never once came to see you during that time?'

'No. Although it was my birthday last week. He sent me some flowers.'

'Where did he send them from?'

'An errand boy brought them.'

'Was there no florist's name on them?'

'There may have been. I didn't look.'

'You didn't recognize the errand boy? He wasn't from hereabouts?'

'I'd never seen him before.'

He did not ask to search Honoré Cuendet's room for clues. He was only there unofficially. He had not been put in charge of the investigation.

Inspector Fumel would no doubt be coming along presently, armed with a proper warrant, signed by the examining magistrate. He would probably find nothing. On previous occasions Maigret himself had found nothing, except a neat row of suits, linen on the wardrobe shelves, a few books, and some tools which were not burglar's implements.

'How long was it since he'd last vanished in that way?'

She searched her memory. Her mind was not entirely on the conversation and she had to make an effort.

'He was here nearly all winter.'

'And in the summer?'

'I don't know where he went then.'

'He didn't suggest taking you away to the country or the seaside?'

'I wouldn't have gone. I've lived too much in the country to want to go back there.'

She must have been about fifty, or a little over, when she first discovered Paris, and the only town she had known before that was Lausanne.

She came from Sénarclens, a tiny hamlet in the canton of Vaud, near a village called Cossonay, where her husband worked as a farm labourer.

Maigret had passed quickly through that part of the country once, long ago, on holiday with his wife, and the inns were what he remembered best.

And it was precisely those clean, quiet inns that had been the ruin of Gilles Cuendet – a little bandy-legged, taciturn man who would sit for hours in a corner, drinking glass after glass of white wine.

From being a farm labourer he had sunk to the level of mole-catcher, going from farm to farm to set his traps, and people declared he stank as badly as his quarry.

The couple had two children, Honoré and his sister Laurence. The girl had been sent to Geneva to work as a barmaid, had ended by marrying someone from Unesco – a translator, if Maigret remembered rightly – and had gone to South America with him.

'Have you any news of your daughter?'

'She sent me a Christmas card. She has five children now. I'll show you the card.'

She went to the next room to fetch it, more as an excuse for moving about than to convince Maigret.

The card showed Rio bay in the glow of a red and purple sunset.

'Does she never write you more than that?'

'Why should she? We're on opposite sides of the ocean, we shall never see each other again. She's made her own life, after all.'

So had Honoré, but differently. At the age of fifteen he, too, had been sent away to work, apprenticed to a locksmith at Lausanne.

He was a placid, secretive boy, scarcely more talkative than his father. He had an attic room in an old house near the market-place, and it was there that the police suddenly appeared one morning as the result of an anonymous denunciation. At that time Honoré was not yet seventeen. They had found all sorts of things in his room, a jumble of incongruous objects the origin of which he had not even attempted to explain – alarm clocks, tools, tinned foods, children's clothes with the price-tags still on them, two or three wireless sets that he had not even unpacked.

At first the police thought he was a 'pull-in' thief, stealing from parked lorries.

Investigation revealed, however, that he was nothing of the kind – that he used to break into closed shops, warehouses and empty flats and carry off indiscriminately whatever he could lay hands on.

As he was so young they had sent him to the approved school at Vennes, above Lausanne, where he had been given his choice of several trades and had elected to be trained as a boiler-maker.

For a year he had been a model pupil, quiet, good-mannered, hard-working and always obedient to the rules.

Then he suddenly vanished without trace: and ten years were to go by before Maigret ran across him in Paris.

The first thing he had done on leaving Switzerland – where he never set foot again – was to enlist in the Foreign Legion, and he had spent five years at Sidi-Bel-Abbès and in Indo-China.

The superintendent had had occasion to study his military record and to have a chat with one of his superior officers.

There again, Honoré Cuendet had been, by and large, a model soldier. The only complaint was that he was unsociable, had no friends and never mixed with the others even on festive occasions.

'He was a soldier the way another man might be a fitter or a cobbler,' said his lieutenant.

He went through three years without a single punishment. Whereupon, for no known reason, he deserted, and was discovered after a few days in a workshop in Algiers, where he had found a job.

He offered no explanation of his abrupt departure, which might have got him into considerable trouble, beyond a muttered:

'I couldn't stand it any longer.'

'Why not?'

'I don't know.'

Thanks to his three years of irreproachable service he was let off lightly. Six months later he ran away again, and this time was caught after only twenty-four hours of freedom, in a lorry where he was hiding among a load of vegetables.

It was in the Legion that, at his own request, a fish had been tattooed on his left arm; Maigret had tried to find out why. Most Legionaries prefer more suggestive designs.

It was a man of twenty-six who had confronted Maigret on that first occasion, a shortish, broad-shouldered man with carroty hair.

'Have you ever seen any sea-horses?'

'Not live ones.'

'Any dead ones?'

'One, once.'

'Where?'

'At Lausanne.'

'Where at Lausanne?'

'In a woman's room.'

The words had to be dragged out of him one by one, as it were.

'Who was the woman?'

'A woman I went to see.'

'Before you were shut up at Vennes?'

'Yes.'

'You followed her?'

'Yes.'

'In the street?'

'Yes, right down the Rue Centrale.'

'And there was a dried sea-horse in her room?'

'That's right. She told me it was her mascot.'

'Have you known a lot of other women?'

'Not a great many.'

Maigret thought he understood.

'What did you do when you were demobbed from the Legion and came to Paris?'

'I worked.'

'Where?'

'At a locksmith's in the Rue de la Roquette.'

The police had checked this statement and found it to be true. He had worked there for two years and given entire satisfaction. True, his mates teased him for being 'standoffish', but he was regarded as a model workman.

'What did you do in the evenings?'

'Nothing.'

'Didn't you go to the cinema?'

'Hardly ever.'

'Had you any men friends?'

'No.'

'Any girl friends?'

'Not likely!'

It looked as though women scared him. And yet it was because of the first woman he had ever met, when he was only sixteen, that he'd had a sea-horse tattooed on his arm.

The inquiry had been very thorough. In those days there was time to be fussy. Maigret was still a mere inspector, and only about three years older than Cuendet.

It had happened in rather the same way as at Lausanne, except that on this occasion there had been no anonymous letter.

Very early one morning – about four o'clock, in fact, like the discovery of the body in the Bois de Boulogne – a constable in uniform had spoken to a man who was carrying a large parcel. It happened quite by accident. But for a second the man had made as if to run away.

The parcel contained fur-skins, and Cuendet refused to account for his strange burden.

'Where were you going with all that?'

'I don't know.'

'Where have you come from?'

'I have nothing to say.'

In the end they had discovered that the skins belonged to a furrier who worked in his own flat in the Rue des Francs-Bourgeois.

Cuendet was then living in a furnished room in the Rue Saint-Antoine, a hundred yards from the Place de la Bastille; and there, just as in his attic at Lausanne, the police had found a large and varied assortment of goods.

'Who were you selling the stuff to?'

'Nobody.'

That seemed highly unlikely; but it proved impossible to discover any evidence of complicity between the Swiss youth and the known receivers of stolen goods.

He had little money on him. His expenditure tallied with the wages his employer paid him.

Maigret had found the case so intriguing that he had persuaded his superior, Superintendent Guillaume, to ask for a medical report on the prisoner.

'He's certainly what we call an asocial type,' said the doctor, 'but he seems to me to have rather more than average intelligence and quite normal emotional reactions.'

Cuendet had the good luck to be defended by a young barrister who later became one of the stars of the profession – Maître Gambier, thanks to whom he was given the minimum sentence.

After an initial period in the Santé prison, Cuendet had spent a little more than a year at Fresnes, where his behaviour had, as usual, been exemplary, so that several months of his sentence were remitted.

In the meantime his father had been killed – knocked down by a car one evening when he was riding home dead drunk on a bicycle with no lights.

Honoré had induced his mother to leave Sénarclens for Paris, so that after living all her life in the quietest corner of the European countryside, she had suddenly found herself transplanted to the noisy, crowded Rue Mouffetard.

She too was phenomenal in her way. Instead of being terrified and taking a dislike to the great city, she had settled down so completely into her district and her street that she had become one of its most popular characters.

Her name was Justine, and by now everybody from end to end of the Rue Mouffetard knew old Justine, with her slow speech and twinkling eyes.

The fact that her son had done time did not disturb her in the least.

'There's no accounting for tastes or opinions,' she used to say.

Maigret had had dealings with Honoré Cuendet on two subsequent occasions, the second time as the result of a big jewel robbery in the Rue de la Pompe, at Passy.

The burglary had occurred in a luxury flat while the owners and their servants were asleep. The jewels had been left that evening on a dressing-table in the boudoir next to the owners' bedroom, and the door between the two rooms had remained open all night.

Neither Monsieur nor Madame D. had heard a sound to disturb their sleep. The housemaid, who slept on the same floor, was positive that she had bolted the front door and found it bolted the following morning. There were no signs of forced entry and no fingerprints.

It was a third-floor flat, so nobody could have climbed in through a window. And there was no balcony along which a burglar could have made his way from a neighbouring flat.

This was the fifth or sixth such robbery within three years, and the papers were beginning to talk about a 'phantom burglar'.

Maigret remembered that spring and how the Rue de la Pompe had looked at all hours of the day; for he had gone from door to door, tirelessly questioning everybody – not only the concierges and shopkeepers, but the residents and their servants.

It was thus, by accident, or rather by sheer persistence, that he had come across Cuendet. In the house opposite the scene of the robbery there had been a room to let, six weeks before – an attic overlooking the street.

'Such a nice, quiet gentleman has taken it,' said the concierge. 'He goes out very little, never at night, and never has women up to see him. Nor anyone else, for that matter.'

'He looks after the room himself?'

'Indeed he does. And I can assure you he keeps it clean.'

Was Cuendet so sure of himself that he had not bothered to move after the burglary? Or had he been afraid that to give up his room would arouse suspicion?

Maigret had found him at home, reading. Looking out of the window, he discovered that he could watch the occupants of the flats across the road in their comings and goings.

'I must ask you to accompany me to the headquarters of the Judicial Police.'

The Swiss had made no protest. Without a word he had allowed his room to be searched. Nothing had been found – not one piece of jewellery, not one skeleton key, not one cat-burglar's tool.

His interrogation at the Quai des Orfèvres had lasted nearly twenty-four hours, with pauses for beer and sandwiches.

'Why did you rent that room?'

'Because I liked it.'

'Have you quarrelled with your mother?'

'No.'

'But you don't live with her any more?'

'I shall go back one day.'

'You have left nearly all your belongings there.'

'Exactly.'

'Have you been to see her lately?'

'No.'

'Who have you seen?'

'The concierge, the neighbours, people going along the street.'

These replies were given in a tone that was slightly ironical – unintentionally so, perhaps, for Cuendet's face remained placid and grave and he seemed to be doing his very best to satisfy the superintendent.

The interrogation had led to nothing, but inquiries in the Rue Mouffetard had produced some circumstantial evidence, revealing that this was not the first time Honoré had vanished for longish periods – usually from three weeks to two months – after which he would return to his mother's roof.

'What do you live on?'

'I do odd jobs, and I have a little put by.'

'In the bank?'

'No. I don't trust banks.'

'Where is this money?'

He did not reply. Since his first arrest he had studied the Criminal Code and knew it by heart.

'It's not for me to prove that I am innocent. It's for you to show that I'm guilty.'

Only once had Maigret lost his temper, and Cuendet's air of mild reproof had made him regret it immediately.

'You got rid of the jewels somehow or other. Probably you sold them. To whom?'

Naturally the police had gone the rounds of the known receivers, given the alarm in Antwerp, Amsterdam and London. They had tipped the wink to their informers as well.

Nobody knew Cuendet. Nobody had seen him. Nobody had been in touch with him.

'What did I tell you?' his mother exclaimed jubilantly. 'I know you're a clever lot, but my son is an exceptional man!'

In spite of his past record, in spite of the attic room, in spite of the circumstantial evidence, they had been compelled to let him go.

Cuendet had shown no elation. He had taken it all calmly. Maigret could still see him, looking for his hat, pausing at the door, extending a hesitant hand as he said:

'*Au revoir*, superintendent . . .'

As though he quite expected to come back another time!

# Chapter Three

The straw-bottomed chairs gleamed like copper in the dim light. Though the floor-boards were ordinary pitch-pine, and very old at that, they were so well polished that the rectangle of the window was reflected in them. There was a wall clock with a brass pendulum that swung gently to and fro.

Even the most trivial objects – the poker, the china bowls with their pattern of big pink flowers, even the broom against which the cat was now rubbing his back – seemed to have a life of their own, such as one senses in old Dutch paintings, or in a church vestry.

The old woman opened the stove and threw in two shovelfuls of shiny coal, and for a second the flames leapt out at her face.

'May I take off my overcoat?'

'Does that mean you're going to stay a long time?'

'It's well below freezing-point out of doors, and this room is on the warm side.'

'They say old folks feel the cold,' she muttered, speaking more for herself, to occupy her mind, than for him. 'But my stove keeps me company. My son was the same, even as a boy. I can still see him in our cottage at Sénarclens, sitting right up against the stove while he did his homework.'

She looked at the empty armchair with its polished wood and shabby leather upholstery.

'Here too, he'd draw that chair up to the stove and spend the whole day reading, not hearing anything that went on.'

'What used he to read?'

She raised her arms with a helpless gesture.

'How should I know? He used to get books from the lending library in the Rue Monge. Here's the last he took out. He changed them as he went along. He had some kind of subscription. I expect you've read this one . . .'

The volume, bound in black cloth that had been rubbed shiny like a worn cassock, proved to be a book by Lenôtre on an episode during the French Revolution.

'He knew a great deal, Honoré did. He wasn't a great talker but his brain never stopped working. He used to read newspapers too, four or five a day, and thick expensive magazines with coloured pictures . . .'

Maigret liked the smell of the flat, a mixture of many different smells. He had always had a weakness for houses with a distinctive smell, and now he was hesitant about lighting his pipe, which he had filled automatically.

'Smoke if you like. He used to smoke a pipe too. In fact he was so fond of some of his old pipes that he used to mend them with wire.'

'There's something I would like to ask you, Madame Cuendet.'

'It makes me feel so strange when you call me that. Everybody's been calling me Justine for such a long time now! I don't really believe anyone has ever called me anything else, except the mayor when he gave me his good wishes after my wedding. But ask your question. I'll answer it if I feel inclined.'

'You don't work. Your husband was a poor man . . .'

'Did you ever meet a rich mole-catcher? Especially one who drank from morning to night?'

'So you are living on what your son has been giving you.'

'Anything wrong about that?'

'A workman hands over his weekly wages to his wife or his mother; a clerk gives her his monthly salary. I suppose Honoré used to give you money as and when you needed it?'

She looked searchingly at him, as though she grasped the implications of his question.

'And so . . . ?'

'He may also have given you large sums – after each of his absences, for instance.'

'There has never been a large sum in this place. What would I have done with it?'

'He was sometimes away for quite a time, even for weeks on end, wasn't he? If you ran short of money at such times, what used you to do?'

'I never ran short.'

'He gave you enough before he left?'

'To say nothing of the fact that I have accounts at the butcher's and the grocer's and that I can buy on credit from any of the shops around here, or even from the barrow-boys. Everybody in this street knows old Justine.'

'He never sent you a money-order?'

'I shouldn't have known how to cash it.'

'Listen, Madame Cuendet . . .'

'I would really rather you called me Justine . . .'

She was standing up; she added a little hot water to her stew and replaced the lid, leaving a narrow opening for the steam to escape.

'I can't give him any more trouble now, and I've no intention of giving you any. All I want is to find the man who killed him.'

'When can I see him?'

'This afternoon, I expect. An inspector will call for you.'

'And will they give him back to me?'

'I think they will. In order to catch his murderer, or murderers, I need to know certain things.'

'What do you want to know?'

Even now she was wary, like the peasant she had remained at heart, like any almost illiterate old woman, scenting a trap at every turn. She couldn't help it.

'Your son used to leave you several times a year, sometimes staying away for several weeks . . .'

'Sometimes it was three weeks, sometimes two months.'

'What was he like when he came back?'

'Like a man who's glad to be home by his own fire.'

'Used he to tell you he was going away, or did he simply leave without a word?'

'Who would have packed for him, in that case?'

'Well then, he used to tell you. He took away a change of clothes, of underwear . . .'

'He took all a man needs.'

'He had several suits?'

'Four or five; he liked to be well dressed.'

'Is it your impression that when he got back he used to hide anything in the flat?'

'It wouldn't be easy to find a hiding-place in these four rooms. Besides, you searched them – more than once. I remember your men poking about everywhere; they even took my furniture to pieces. They went down to the cellar, though it's shared by all the tenants, and up to the corner of the loft that we're allowed to use.'

That was true, and they had found nothing.

'Your son had no bank account, we made sure of that, and no savings account. But he must have put his money somewhere. Do you know if he ever went abroad – to Belgium, for instance, or to Switzerland or Spain?'

'In Switzerland he'd have been arrested.'

'Quite true.'

'He never spoke to me about the other countries you mentioned.'

The frontiers had been warned on several occasions. For years a photograph of Honoré Cuendet had been among those of the people to be watched for at frontier railway stations and other points of departure from France.

Maigret continued, thinking aloud:

'Obviously he must have sold some of the jewels and other stuff. He never went to professional receivers. And as he spent very little, he's bound to have had a large sum in one place or another.'

He looked more closely at the old woman.

'If he only gave you housekeeping money when you needed it, what will become of you now?'

This idea struck her, and she jumped slightly. He saw a flicker of anxiety in her eyes. But she answered proudly, 'I'm not frightened. Honoré's a good son.'

This time she did not say 'was'. And she went on, as though he were still alive, 'I'm sure he won't leave me without a penny.'

Maigret pursued his reflections:

'He wasn't killed by a tramp. He wasn't killed by a thief. And he wasn't killed by an accomplice.'

She did not ask him how he knew, and he didn't explain. A prowling tramp would have had no reason for smashing up the dead man's face or for emptying his pockets completely, even down to odd scraps of paper, pipe and matches.

Nor would an accomplice have done that, for he would have known that Cuendet had been in prison and could therefore be identified by his fingerprints.

'The man who killed him didn't know him. And yet he had some important reason for getting rid of him. You understand?'

'What am I supposed to understand?'

'That once we know what job Honoré was planning, what house or flat he had got himself into, we shall be well on the way to finding out who murdered him.'

'That won't bring him back to life.'

'May I take a look at his room?'

'I can't stop you.'

'I would rather you came with me.'

She followed him, shrugging her thin shoulders, rolling her almost deformed hips; and the little sandy dog trotted behind, ready to start growling again.

The dining-room was lifeless, expressionless, there was hardly even a smell about it. In the old woman's room the iron bed was covered with an immaculately white bedspread. Honoré's room, which looked on to the courtyard and was rather dark, already seemed to have a suggestion of death about it.

Opening the wardrobe, Maigret saw three suits hanging there – two grey and one navy blue – with a row of shoes along the bottom and a shelf piled with shirts, on top of which lay a bunch of dried lavender.

There was a bookcase containing a red-bound, battered copy of the Penal Code, which must have been bought from one of the secondhand book dealers along the Seine or up the Boulevard Saint-Michel; a few early twentieth-century novels, a volume of Zola and one of Tolstoy, and a much-thumbed plan of Paris.

In a corner, on a small table with a shelf below it, lay some magazines whose titles made the superintendent raise his eyebrows. They did not square with the rest. They were thick, expensive 'glossies', with colour photographs of some of the finest country houses in France and of certain sumptuous Paris flats.

Maigret leafed through a few of them, hoping to find notes or pencil markings.

In his young days as a locksmith's apprentice at Lausanne, Cuendet had lived in a garret and picked up whatever came to hand, including quite worthless objects.

Later, living in the Rue Saint-Antoine, he had shown rather more discrimination, but he still confined himself to haphazard pilfering from local shops and flats.

Then he moved up a step and set to work on middle-class homes, where he found money and jewellery.

Finally, by dint of patience, he had made his way into the fashionable districts. Just now, the old woman had unintentionally given away something important by mentioning that her son read four or five daily newspapers.

Maigret would have been ready to bet that Cuendet didn't read them for their news items, let alone for their political articles, but for their society columns with announcements of weddings, accounts of receptions and first nights.

For these included descriptions of the jewels worn by smart women.

The magazines at which Maigret was now glancing contained information of equal value to Honoré – meticulous descriptions of private mansions and flats, with photographs of individual rooms.

Cuendet used to sit by the fire, musing, weighing the pros and cons, making his choice.

Then he would prowl round the district and take a room in a hotel – or, if he could find one to let, in a private house, as in the case of the Rue de la Pompe.

At the last inquiry, several years ago, they had picked up his trail in this way, finding that he had become a sudden and temporary habitué of various local cafés.

A quiet man who used to sit for hours in his favourite corner, drinking white wine, reading the papers and watching the scene outside . . .

So that after a time a whole block of flats would have revealed its every secret to him.

'Thank you, Madame Cuendet.'

'Justine!'

'Excuse me – Justine. I used to feel very . . .'

He sought for the right word. 'Friendly' was too strong. 'Drawn towards' she wouldn't understand.

'I had a great regard for your son.'

That was not quite what he meant, either; but the deputy

prosecutor and the examining magistrate were not there to overhear him.

'Inspector Fumel will be coming to see you. If there is anything you need, get in touch with me.'

'I shan't need anything.'

'If you happen to discover whereabouts in Paris Honoré spent these last few weeks . . .'

He put on his heavy overcoat and went cautiously down the worn stairs and out into the cold, noisy street. By this time there was a suggestion of white powder floating in the air, but it was not snowing and there were no signs of snow on the ground.

When Maigret entered the inspectors' office, Lucas said:

'Moers rang you.'

'He didn't say why?'

'He asked if you would ring back.'

'Still no news of Fernand?'

He had not forgotten that his main job was to catch the hold-up gang. It might take weeks, even months. Hundreds and thousands of police in Paris and the provinces were carrying the photograph of the newly released prisoner. Inspectors were going from house to house like vacuum-cleaner salesmen, asking: 'Excuse me, madame, but have you seen this man recently?'

The hotel squad was dealing with the lodging-houses. The vice squad was questioning prostitutes. In the railway stations, travellers were being scrutinized, unawares, by watchful eyes.

Maigret was not in charge of the Cuendet inquiry. He had no right to take his men off their other work. But he found a way of reconciling duty with curiosity.

'Go upstairs and ask for a photo of Cuendet, the most recent they've got. Have copies of it given to all the men who are looking for Fernand, particularly those who are making the round of the bistros and lodging-houses.'

'All over Paris?'

He hesitated, on the verge of replying, 'Only in the fashion-able districts.'

But he remembered that private mansions and blocks of luxury flats were to be found in the old districts as well.

Back in his own office, he rang through to Moers.

'Found something?'

'I don't know if it's any use to you. When they went over the clothes with a magnifying-glass, my fellows picked up three or four hairs which they put under the microscope. Delage, who knows his job, assures me they are wild-cat's hairs.'

'Whereabouts on the clothes were they found?'

'On the back, near the left shoulder. There were specks of face powder as well. We may be able to discover what make it is, but that'll take longer.'

'Thank you. Fumel hasn't rung you up?'

'He looked in just now. I gave him the tip.'

'Where is he?'

'In Records, deep in Cuendet's file.'

Maigret wondered for a moment why his eyes felt sore; then he remembered he had been called out of bed at four o'clock that morning.

He had to sign some papers, fill in several forms, and see two people who had been waiting, to whom he listened rather absentmindedly. As soon as he was alone again he telephoned to a big furrier's in the Rue La Boétie, where it needed some persistence to get the proprietor himself at the end of the line.

'I am Superintendent Maigret of the Judicial Police. I apolo-gize for bothering you, but I'd like you to give me a piece of information. Can you tell me approximately how many wild-cat fur coats there are in Paris?'

'Wild-cat?'

The man sounded rather annoyed by the question.

'We have none here. At one time, during the pioneer days of motoring, our firm did make them – some for ladies, but mostly for men.'

Maigret recollected some photographs of early motorists, looking like bears.

'Those were wild-cat?'

'Not all of them, but the finest were. They are still worn by some people in very cold countries – Canada, Sweden, Norway, the north of the United States . . .'

'There are none left in Paris?'

'I believe some firms still sell one occasionally, but very few. It's difficult to give you a definite figure. But I would be willing to bet there are fewer than five hundred such coats in the whole of Paris, and most of those must be fairly old. But . . .'

He had had an idea.

'Is it only coats that interest you?'

'Why do you ask?'

'Because we do, very occasionally, make up wild-cat skins for other purposes. For instance, they are made into rugs to cover a sofa or to take in cars.'

'Are there many of those?'

'If I went through our books I could tell you how many we've turned out in the last few years. At a rough guess, three or four dozen. But they are mass-produced by some furriers – in a cheaper quality, of course. Wait a minute; I've thought of something else. While we were talking I remembered that in the window of a chemist's shop not far from here there is a wild-cat's skin, offered as a cure for rheumatism.'

'Thank you very much.'

'Would you like me to get you a list of the . . .'

'If it's not too much trouble.'

This was rather disheartening. For weeks the police had been hunting for Fernand, though they were not even certain he was implicated in the recent hold-ups. That represented almost as much work as would be needed to prepare a dictionary, for instance, or even an encyclopedia.

And yet they knew all about Fernand, his tastes, his habits and his quirks. For instance there was one trivial detail that might help them to catch him – the only thing he ever drank was Mandarin-Curaçao.

But so far, the only clue that might lead to Cuendet's murderers was a few wild-cat hairs.

Moers had said they were found on the back of the jacket, near the sleeve. If they had come from a coat, wouldn't they have been more likely to be on the front of the suit?

Maigret preferred the theory of the rug, more especially a motor-car rug. In which case the car would not have been a small, ordinary one; fur rugs are seldom found in 4 h.p. Renaults.

And for some years past, Cuendet had confined himself to stealing from wealthy houses.

What was really needed was to go the round of all the garages in Paris, putting the same question to every one of them.

Someone knocked on the door. It was Inspector Fumel, with a puffy face and red eyelids. He had had even less sleep than Maigret. In fact, having been on duty the night before, he had had none at all.

'Am I disturbing you?'

'Come in.'

Fumel was one of the few whom Maigret addressed by the familiar 'tu'. Most of these had been in the force for many years, as long as he himself, and had originally spoken to him with the same familiarity, though now they were shy and called him 'superintendent' or sometimes 'chief'. Another was Lucas. Not Janvier, though Maigret couldn't have said why not. And then the very young ones such as little Lapointe.

'Sit down.'

'I've been through the whole file. And now I don't know how to set about the job. A team of twenty men wouldn't be enough. I see from the minutes of the interrogations that you knew him well.'

'Pretty well. This morning I paid an unofficial call on his mother. I broke the news to her and said you'd go round presently and take her to the Medico-Legal Institute. Have you any information about the results of the post-mortem?'

'None. I rang up Doctor Lamalle. He informed me, through his assistant, that he'd be sending his report to the examining magistrate tonight or tomorrow morning.'

Doctor Paul used not to wait for Maigret to ring him up. And sometimes he would even inquire gruffly:

'What am I to tell the magistrate?'

In those days, of course, investigations were left to the police, and the examining magistrate didn't usually take over until the criminal had confessed.

At that time a case used to be taken in three separate stages: the investigation, which in Paris was the responsibility of the Quai des Orfèvres; the examination of the evidence; and later, when the file had been studied by the Grand Jury, the actual trial.

'Did Moers tell you about the hairs?'

'Yes. Wild-cat's hairs.'

'I've telephoned to a furrier. You'd better look into the sales of wild-cat fur rugs in Paris. And if you question the garage-keepers . . .'

'I'm alone on this job.'

'I know, old man.'

'I've sent in my preliminary report. Maître Cajou wants to see me at five o'clock this afternoon. There'll be a row about that. As I was on duty last night I should have been free today, and somebody's expecting me. I shall ring up, but I know I shan't be believed, and it'll cause no end of complications . . .'

A woman, of course!

'If I come across anything, I'll give you a ring,' said Maigret. 'But for heaven's sake don't tell the examining magistrate that I'm dealing with the business.'

'Right!'

Maigret went home to lunch. The flat was as clean as old Madame Cuendet's, the floors and the furniture as well polished.

It was warm, too, and there was a stove burning, in spite of the central heating. Maigret had always been fond of stoves, and had long ago persuaded the administration to leave him one in his office.

There was a good smell of cooking. And yet he suddenly felt that something was missing, though he couldn't have said what.

The atmosphere of Honoré's mother's flat had been even more soothing, more pervasive, perhaps in contrast to the busy street outside. From the window one could almost touch the pavement stalls, and their owners' cries were clearly audible.

The ceilings in that flat were lower, the place was smaller and more withdrawn. The old woman spent her entire time there. And although Honoré was away, one felt conscious that he belonged there.

Maigret wondered for a moment whether he, too, should not buy a dog and a cat.

What nonsense! He wasn't an old woman, nor a country boy come to Paris to live alone in its most crowded street.

'A penny for your thoughts!'

He smiled. 'I was thinking about a dog.'

'Are you planning to buy one?'

'No. Besides, it wouldn't be the same. This one was picked up in the street with two broken legs . . .'

'Aren't you going to take a nap?'

'No time, unfortunately.'

'You seem to be thinking about something that's partly nice and partly nasty . . .'

He was struck by the discernment of this remark. Cuendet's death had left him depressed and mortified. He felt a personal grudge against the murderers, as though Honoré had been a friend, a colleague, or at any rate an old acquaintance.

And he hated the way they had disfigured the man and thrown him out, like a dead animal, beside a path in the Bois des Boulogne where his body must have bounced on the frozen ground.

Yet at the same time he couldn't help laughing when he thought of the life Cuendet had led, and of the man's whims, which he was now trying to understand. It was a funny thing but, although the two of them were so unalike, he had the impression that he was succeeding.

It was true that, at the beginning of his career, if one could call it that, when he was only a skinny apprentice, Honoré had developed his skill by the most commonplace means, indiscriminately pinching whatever came to hand, like all juvenile delinquents born in poor districts.

He had not even sold his spoils, just stacked them in his attic, the way a puppy hides crusts of bread and old bones under its rug.

Why, when he was regarded as a model soldier, had he twice deserted? Clumsily! Stupidly! On both occasions he had let himself be recaptured, with no attempt to run away or resist.

In Paris, when he lived near the Bastille, he had improved his technique and his individual style had begun to take shape. He did not join a gang. He had no friends. He worked on his own.

Locksmith, coppersmith, handyman, clever with his hands, a careful workman, he was learning how to break into shops, workshops and warehouses.

He was unarmed. He had never possessed a weapon, not even a flick-knife.

Not once had he set off an alarm, or left trace of his passage. He was an essentially silent man, in his work as well as in private life.

What were his relations with women? There were none in evidence in his life. He had always lived under his mother's roof, and if he had occasional brief affairs he must have conducted them discreetly, in remote districts where no one noticed him.

He was capable of sitting for hours in some café, next to the window, with a small pitcher of white wine in front of him. He was also capable of spending whole days watching from the window of a furnished room, or reading beside the fire in the Rue Mouffetard.

His needs were very few. But the list of jewels he had stolen – to speak only of the thefts that could reasonably be placed at his door – represented a fortune.

Did he pass some of his time away from Paris, living in a different style and spending his money?

'I'm thinking about a funny sort of chap, a burglar...' Maigret explained to his wife.

'The one who was murdered last night?'

'How did you know?'

'It's in the midday edition of the paper; somebody brought me one just now.'

'Show me.'

'It's only a few lines. I came across it by accident.'

MAN'S BODY FOUND IN THE BOIS DE BOULOGNE
About three o'clock this morning, two constables of the 16th *arrondissement* cycle patrol found a man's body beside a path in the Bois de Boulogne. The skull had been shattered. The man was identified as Honoré Cuendet, an ex-convict of Swiss

nationality. Monsieur Cajou, the examining magistrate, who went to the spot, accompanied by Monsieur Kernavel, of the Public Prosecutor's Department, and by the police doctor, believes the man to have been killed in an underworld vendetta.

'What did you say?'

The stock phrase 'underworld vendetta' infuriated Maigret, for it meant that from the official standpoint the matter was as good as closed. As one of the Public Prosecutor's men used to say:

'Let 'em kill one another, down to the last man. That'll save the hangman trouble and the taxpayers money.'

'What was I saying? Oh yes! Imagine a burglar who deliberately chose occupied houses and flats . . .'

'To break into?'

'Yes. Every year and at every season, so to speak, there are flats in Paris which are left empty for weeks at a time, while their owners are at the seaside, at winter sports, in their country houses, or travelling abroad.'

'And they're burgled, aren't they?'

'Yes, they are. By specialists who will never go near a house where they're liable to run into anybody.'

'What are you getting at?'

'At the fact that my friend Cuendet was only interested in occupied flats. He would often wait to break into a place until the owners were back from the theatre or wherever they'd gone, and the wife had taken off her jewels and put them in the next-door room or even, sometimes, left them lying somewhere in the bedroom itself.'

To which the practical Madame Maigret replied:

'If he'd done his job while she was out he wouldn't have found her jewels, since you say she would be wearing them.'

'He'd probably have found others, and in any case there would be valuables, pictures and money.'

'You mean it was a kind of vice he had?'

'That's too strong a word, perhaps; but I suspect it was a mania, that he got some kind of pleasure out of worming his way into the warmth of other people's lives. Once he took a man's watch off his bedside table, while the fellow slept on and didn't hear a sound.'

She, too, laughed at this.

'How often did you catch him?'

'He was only sent to prison once, and in those days he hadn't adopted this system, he worked just like any other burglar. All the same, at the office we have a long list of burglaries which were almost certainly done by him. In some cases he'd rented a room opposite the burgled house for several weeks, and couldn't give any plausible explanation.'

'Why was he murdered?'

'That's what I'm wondering. In order to find out, I need to discover what house he burgled lately – probably last night.'

Maigret had seldom told his wife so much about a case while it was in progress; perhaps because for him this was no ordinary case, and he wasn't even in charge of it.

Cuendet interested him as a person and as an expert – had almost a kind of fascination for him, and so had old Justine.

'*I'm sure he won't leave me without a penny,*' she had declared confidently.

Yet Maigret felt certain she didn't know where her son used to hide the money.

She had confidence, unreasoning trust: Honoré was incapable of leaving her unprovided for.

How would the money get to her? What arrangements had her son made – he who had never in his life worked with an accomplice?

And how could he have foreseen that he would be murdered one day?

The strange thing was that Maigret was beginning to share

the old woman's confidence, her conviction that Cuendet would have thought of every eventuality.

He sipped his coffee slowly. In the act of lighting his pipe, he glanced towards the sideboard. Like the one in the Rue Mouffetard, it held a bottle of white spirits – plum brandy in this particular case.

Madame Maigret interpreted the glance and poured him out a small glass.

# Chapter Four

At five minutes to four, Maigret, bending over an annotated file that lay in the circle of light thrown by his lamp, was hesitating between two pipes when the telephone rang. It was the Emergency Calls exchange in the Boulevard du Palais.

'A hold-up in the Rue La Fayette, between the Rue Taitbout and the Chaussée d'Antin. Some shots were fired. Several casualties . . .'

The thing had happened at ten minutes to four, and already the general alarm had been given, the radio cars alerted, and a bus-load of uniformed police was leaving the courtyard of the Municipal Police headquarters while, in obedience to the Public Prosecutor's orders, the news was being transmitted to him in his tranquil office in the Palais de Justice.

Maigret opened the door, beckoned to Janvier and muttered something indistinct. The two men hurried downstairs, struggling into their overcoats, and jumped into one of the small black-and-white police cars.

A yellowish fog had begun to settle down on the city soon after lunch, so that it was now as dark as at six in the evening, and the cold had become more penetrating instead of diminishing.

'Tomorrow morning it'll be as well to look out for ice on the roads,' the driver observed.

He started his siren and switched on his winking headlight. Taxis and private cars drew in to the kerb, and pedestrians stared after the police car. Signs of traffic disturbance were evident by the time they reached the Place de l'Opéra. Bottle-necks had formed. The extra police who had come on point duty were blowing their whistles and gesticulating.

The rush-hour had begun, and in the Rue La Fayette, along the pavement outside the Galeries Lafayette and the Galeries du Printemps, there was a dense crowd, composed chiefly of women: this was also the most brightly lit spot in Paris.

The crowd was being shepherded behind the barricades which had been set up. A length of the street was empty except for the dark figures of a few officials, going to and fro.

The superintendent of police of the 9th *arrondissement* had arrived, with several of his men. Experts were taking measure-ments and making chalk-marks. A car stood with its front wheels on the pavement: its windscreen was shattered and two or three yards away there was a dark patch with a group of men standing round it talking in low voices.

A little grey-haired man in black, with a knitted muffler round his neck, stood there, still holding the glass of rum they had brought him from the café across the street. He was the cashier of a big ironmonger's in the Rue de Châteaudun.

For the third or fourth time he was retelling his story, his eyes carefully averted from a human form that lay a few yards away, with a piece of some rough material thrown over it.

The crowd was pressing against the barrier of portable wooden railings – of the type used in the city along procession routes – and excited women were talking in shrill voices.

'As usual on the last day of the month . . .'

Maigret had forgotten this was January 31.

'. . . I had been to the bank, behind the Opéra, to fetch the money for the staff salaries . . .'

Maigret had often gone past the shop, without realizing how large it was. It had three floors of departments and basements on two levels, and there were three hundred employees.

'I had barely six hundred yards to walk. I was carrying my briefcase in my left hand.'

'It was not chained to your wrist?'

The man was not an official bank messenger, and was not provided with any means of giving an alarm signal. All he had was a revolver, in the right-hand pocket of his overcoat.

He had crossed the street between the yellow lines, and was walking towards the Rue Taitbout, in a crowd so thick that no attack seemed possible. Suddenly he noticed a man walking close beside him; and glancing back, he saw another at his heels.

After that, everything had happened so fast that he had scarcely followed the course of events. What he remembered best was that a voice had muttered in his ear:

'If you want to keep a whole skin, don't try to show off!'

At the same moment the briefcase was wrenched out of his hand. One of the men rushed towards a car that was crawling towards them, close to the kerb. Hearing a shot, the cashier at first thought someone had fired at him. Women were screaming and jostling in the crowd. There was another shot, followed by the tinkle of broken glass.

More shots had followed – some people said three, others four or five.

A red-faced man was standing on one side, with the district superintendent. He looked rather perturbed, not knowing as yet whether he would be treated as a hero or reprimanded.

This was Constable Margeret, of the 1st *arrondissement*. Being off duty this afternoon, he was not in uniform. Then why had he been carrying his revolver? He would have to explain that later.

'I was going to meet my wife, who had been shopping. I saw what happened. When the three men made for the car . . .'

'There were three of them?'

'Yes – one on either side of the cashier and one right behind him . . .'

Constable Margeret had fired. One of the gangsters had fallen on his knees and then sunk slowly to the ground, among the feet of the women who had started to run.

The car drove off at top speed towards Saint-Augustin. The policeman on point duty blew his whistle. Shots were fired from the car, which soon disappeared among the other traffic.

For the next couple of days Maigret had little time to think about his placid Swiss burglar, and on two occasions when Inspector Fumel rang him up he was too busy to take the call.

The police had collected the names and addresses of about fifty eye-witnesses, including a woman who kept a pancake stall near by, a crippled beggar whose pitch was a few yards from the spot, two waiters from the café opposite, and the lady at the pay-desk there – she claimed to have seen all that happened, although the café windows had been steamed up.

There had been a second victim, a man of thirty-five who left a wife and children; he had been killed outright and never realized what was happening.

For the first time since the present series of attacks began, the police had captured a member of the gang – the man shot down by Constable Margeret, who had so miraculously been on the spot.

'My idea was to shoot him in the leg, to stop him from running away.'

In point of fact, however, the man had been hit in the back of the neck, and was now lying in a coma in the Hôpital Beaujon, where he had been taken by ambulance.

Lucas, Janvier and Torrence were taking turns to watch outside his door, waiting till he should be able to make a statement – for the doctors did not despair of saving him.

Next day, as the driver of the police car had predicted, the Paris streets were coated in ice. The light was bad. The traffic crawled along. Municipal lorries scattered sand in the main streets.

The wide corridor of Judicial Police headquarters was full of people waiting in silence. To each of them in turn Maigret patiently put the same questions, while he drew mysterious signs on a plan of the scene which had been drawn up by the appropriate service.

He had gone at once, on the evening of the attack, to Fontenay-aux-Roses, to the address of the wounded gangster, a certain Joseph Raison, described on his identity card as a metal-fitter.

There, in a new building, he had found a bright, trim flat, a fair-haired young woman, and two little girls, aged six and nine, busy with their homework.

Joseph Raison, a man of forty-two, really was a metal-fitter, and worked in a factory on the Quai de Javel. He owned a 2 h.p. Citroën in which he used to take his family for a run in the country every Sunday.

His wife declared that she simply could not understand what had happened, and Maigret believed her.

'I don't see why he should have done such a thing, super-intendent. We were so happy. It's only just two years since we bought this flat. Joseph was earning good wages. He doesn't drink and he hardly ever went out by himself.'

The superintendent had driven her to the hospital, while a neighbour looked after the children. She had seen her husband for a few minutes and then, on doctor's orders and despite her protests, had been driven home again.

And now the mass of confused and contradictory evidence must be sorted out. Some people had seen too much, others too little.

'If I say anything, those chaps will hunt me down . . .'

All the same, it added up to a fairly convincing description of the two men on either side of the cashier, and especially of the one who had grabbed the briefcase.

But it was not until in the afternoon that a witness – one of the café waiters – said he thought he recognized one of the photographs shown to him, which was that of Fernand.

'He came in about ten or fifteen minutes before the attack and ordered a café crème. He was sitting at a table next to the door, right next to the window.'

Two days after the incident, Maigret secured another scrap of evidence: on the 31st, Fernand had been wearing a heavy brown overcoat.

This was not much, but it showed that the superintendent had not been mistaken in supposing that Fernand, lately released from Saint-Martin-de Ré, was the leader of the gang.

The wounded man in the Hôpital Beaujon had regained consciousness for a few moments, but only to whisper:

'Monique . . .'

This was the name of his younger daughter.

Maigret was greatly interested by this new discovery – that Fernand no longer recruited his men solely in the underworld.

The public prosecutor's department was ringing him up at hourly intervals and he was writing one report after another. He could not set foot outside his office without being jumped upon by a swarm of journalists.

At eleven o'clock on the Friday night, the corridor was at last empty. Maigret was talking things over with Lucas, who had just arrived from the Hôpital Beaujon and was telling him that a celebrated surgeon proposed to operate on the wounded man. There was a knock on the door.

'Come in!' called Maigret impatiently.

It was Fumel, who, feeling he had chosen an unpropitious moment, shrank back timidly. He had clearly caught a cold, for his nose was red and his eyes watery.

'I can come back another time . . .'

'Come on in!'

'I think I've found the trail. Or rather the hotel police found it for me. I know where Cuendet had been living the last five weeks.'

For Maigret it was soothing, almost restful, to hear about his placid Swiss burglar.

'Whereabouts was it?'

'In his old district. He'd taken a room in a little hotel in the Rue Neuve Saint-Pierre.'

'Behind the Eglise Saint-Paul?'

This was an ancient, narrow street between the Rue Saint-Antoine and the river. Cars seldom went along it and there were only a few shops.

'Tell me.'

'It seems to be chiefly a house of call for tarts. But they let a few rooms by the month. Cuendet was living there quietly, seldom going out except for meals, which he took at a little restaurant called the Petit Saint-Paul.'

'What's opposite the hotel?'

'An eighteenth-century house with a fine courtyard and tall windows, which was completely restored a few years ago.'

'Who lives there?'

'A lady by herself – with servants, of course. A Mrs Wilton.'

'You've made inquiries about her?'

'I've begun, but the local people know little or nothing.'

In the last ten years or so it had become the fashion for very wealthy people to buy some old house in the Marais – in the Rue des France-Bourgeois, for example – and restore it to more or less its original state.

This had begun with the Île Saint-Louis, and now old mansions were being sought out wherever they still survived, even in the shabbiest streets.

'There's even a tree in the courtyard. One doesn't see many trees in that district.'

'This lady's a widow?'

'Divorced. I went to see a journalist to whom I sometimes

give tips, when it can't do any harm. And this time it was he who gave me one. Although she's divorced she still sees her ex-husband quite often, and they go out together now and again.'

'What's his name?'

'Stuart Wilton. Her maiden name, as I found out from the local police files, was Florence Lenoir. Her mother did ironing at a laundry in the Rue de Rennes, and her father, who died long ago, was in the police. She used to be an actress. According to my journalist she was in a troupe of dancing girls at the Casino de Paris and Stuart Wilton, who had a wife already, got a divorce in order to marry her.'

'How long ago?'

Maigret was doodling on his blotter, seeing a vision of Cuendet at the window of the shady little hotel.

'Ten years, or even less ... The house used to belong to Wilton. He has another, at Auteuil, where he's living at present, and he also owns the Château de Besse, near Maisons-Laffitte.'

'So he keeps racehorses?'

'Not so far as I've heard; he's a keen race-goer, but he doesn't run a stable.'

'Is he American?'

'English. He's been living in France for a very long time.'

'Where does his money come from?'

'I can only pass on what I've been told. He comes of a big manufacturing family and inherited a number of patents that bring him in a lot of money without his raising a finger. He travels for part of the year, rents a villa at Cap d'Antibes or Cap-Ferrat in the summer, and belongs to several clubs. My journalist says he's very well known, but only in a select circle which is hardly ever mentioned in the papers.'

Maigret rose with a sigh, took his coat from its hook, and wound his scarf round his neck.

'Let's get going!' he said; adding, to Lucas:

'If anyone asks for me, I'll be back in an hour.'

Owing to the frost and the icy roads, Paris was almost as deserted as in August, and not a single child was playing in the narrow length of the Rue Neuve Saint-Pierre. The door of the Hôtel Lambert stood ajar; a frosted light-bulb hung above it. In the stuffy office, a man was sitting with his back against the radiator, reading a newspaper.

He recognized Inspector Fumel, and growled as he got to his feet:

'The trouble's beginning, I can see!'

'There'll be no trouble for you if you keep quiet. Is there anyone in Cuendet's room?'

'Not yet. He'd paid the month in advance. I could have let it to someone else on January 31, but as his things were still there I decided to wait.'

'When did he disappear?'

'I don't know. Wait while I calculate. If I'm not mistaken it must have been last Saturday ... Saturday or Friday ... We could ask the chambermaid ...'

'Did he tell you he was going away for a time?'

'He didn't say a word. He was never one for talking, anyhow.'

'Did he go out late on the night of his disappearance?'

'It was my wife who saw him. Customers who bring women here at night don't like to be let in by a man. It embarrasses them. So ...'

'She hasn't mentioned it to you?'

'Indeed she has. Anyway you can ask her presently. She'll soon be down.'

The air was stagnant, overheated, with a vaguely unpleasant smell that had a suggestion of disinfectant, rather like the Métro.

'According to what she told me, he didn't go out to dinner that evening.'

'Was that unusual?'

'It happened now and then. He used to bring food in with

him. We'd see him go upstairs carrying some small parcels and several newspapers. He'd say goodnight and no more would be heard of him till next day.'

'He went out later that evening?'

'He must have, seeing he wasn't in his room the next morning. But so far as that goes, my wife didn't see him. She'd shown a couple upstairs, to a room at the far end of the first-floor corridor. She went to fetch towels for them, and it was then she heard someone going downstairs.'

'What time was that?'

'After midnight. She did mean to look to see who it was, but, by the time she'd shut the linen cupboard and got back to the end of the corridor, the man was already downstairs.'

'When did you discover that he was not in his room?'

'The next morning. It must have been about ten or eleven o'clock when the maid knocked to know if she could do the room. She went in, and saw the bed had not been slept in.'

'You did not inform the police that one of your customers had disappeared?'

'Why should I? He was a free man, wasn't he? He'd paid up. I always make people pay in advance. They're apt to go off like that, without a word . . .'

'Leaving their belongings?'

'He didn't leave much!'

'Take us to his room.'

Dragging his slippered feet, the proprietor shuffled out of the office, behind the two detectives, locked the door and pocketed the key. He was not an old man, but he walked with difficulty and panted as he climbed the stairs.

'It's on the third floor,' he sighed.

There was a pile of sheets on the first-floor landing, and several of the doors along the corridor were open; a servant girl was bustling about in some room or other.

'It's me, Rose. I'm taking some gentlemen upstairs.'

The atmosphere grew staler as they went up, and the third-floor corridor had no carpet. In one of the rooms somebody was playing the mouth-organ.

'Here we are.'

The figure 33 was roughly painted on the door. The room already smelt stuffy.

'I've left everything as it was.'

'Why?'

'I thought he'd be back . . . He looked a decent chap . . . I used to wonder what'd brought him here, seeing he was well dressed and seemed to have plenty of money.'

'How do you know he had money?'

'Both times when he paid, I saw some big notes in his pocket-book.'

'No one ever came to see him?'

'Not to my knowledge, or my wife's. And one or other of us is always in the office.'

'Not at the moment.'

'Well, of course, we do sometimes leave it for a few minutes, but then we listen out, and you'll have noticed I told the chambermaid . . .'

'Did he get any letters?'

'Never.'

'Who's in the next room?'

There was only one, number 33 being at the end of the corridor.

'Olga. A tart.'

The man knew there was no point in trying to hoodwink the police – they were well aware of what went on in his establishment.

'Is she there now?'

'At this time of day she must be asleep.'

'You can go.'

He went off glumly, with his limping gait. Maigret shut the

door and proceeded to open a cheap pitch-pine wardrobe with a weak lock.

There was not much inside – a pair of well-polished black shoes, a pair of slippers, nearly new, and a grey suit on a hanger. There was also a dark felt hat of well-known make.

One drawer held six white shirts, one pale blue one, some underpants, handkerchieves and wool socks. In another were two pairs of pyjamas and several books – *Impressions of a Traveller in Italy*, *Every Man his Own Doctor* (published in 1899) and an adventure story.

The room had an iron bedstead, a round table with a dark green velvet cloth, and one armchair with half its springs broken. The big curtains were stuck and refused to draw, but the light was softened by half-curtains.

Maigret stood and stared at the house opposite, beginning with the courtyard where a big black car of English make was waiting near the steps that led up to the glass-panelled double doors.

The stone façade of the house had been cleaned; it was now a soft shade of grey; there was graceful moulding round the windows.

A lamp was lit in a ground-floor room, its light falling on a carpet with an involved pattern, a Louis XV armchair, and the corner of a small pedestal table.

The first-floor windows were very tall; the floor above was mansard-roofed.

The house was long in proportion to its height, and probably had fewer rooms than one might have supposed at first glance.

Two windows on the first floor stood open, and a manservant in a striped waistcoat was pushing a vacuum cleaner round what looked like a drawing-room.

'Get any sleep last night?' Maigret asked Fumel.

'Yes, chief. I almost had my eight hours.'

'Are you hungry?'

'Not particularly, yet.'

'I'll send someone along presently to relieve you. All you have to do is to sit down in that chair in front of the window. As long as you don't put the light on the people opposite can't see you.'

Wasn't that what Cuendet had been doing for nearly six weeks?

'Make a note of all comings and goings, and if any cars arrive, try to get their numbers.'

A moment later, Maigret was tapping lightly on the door of the next room. He had to wait some time before he heard a bed creak, and then the sound of footsteps. The door opened, but only a crack.

'What is it?'

'Police.'

'Again?' asked the woman, adding resignedly:

'Come in!'

She was in her nightdress, heavy-eyed with sleep. She had not taken off her make-up before going to bed, and it had smeared so that her face looked all askew.

'Mind if I get back into bed?'

'Why did you say "Again"? Have the police been here lately?'

'Not here, but along the street. They've done nothing but pester us for weeks now, and in the last month I've spent at least six nights in the cells. What have I done this time?'

'Nothing, I hope. And please don't tell anybody about my visit.'

'So you're not from the vice squad?'

'No.'

'I seem to have seen your photo somewhere.'

Except for her smears of make-up and her badly dyed hair she would have been quite good-looking; rather plump, but sturdy, and her expression was still alert.

'Superintendent Maigret.'

67

'What's happened?'

'I don't know yet. Have you been living here long?'

'Ever since I came back from Cannes in October. I always do Cannes in the summer.'

'Do you know your neighbour?'

'Which one?'

'The one in number thirty-three.'

'Oh, the Swiss.'

'How do you know he's Swiss?'

'From his accent. I've worked in Switzerland as well – three years ago. I was a hostess in a German nightclub, but they didn't renew my residence permit. I suppose they don't like competition over there.'

'Did he ever speak to you? Did he come to your room?'

'I was the one who went to his. When I got up one afternoon, I found I'd run out of cigarettes. I'd already met him in the passage and he always used to say good-morning, real polite.'

'What happened?'

'Exactly nothing!' she replied, with an expressive grimace. 'I knocked. He took his time opening the door. I wondered what he could be up to. But he was all dressed and there was nobody in his room and it was quite tidy. I saw he was a pipe smoker – he had one in his mouth. I said:

' "I suppose you haven't any cigarettes?"

'He said he was afraid not; and then, kind of hesitating he offered to go and buy me some.

'I was the same as when I opened the door to you – with nothing on but my nightdress. There was some chocolate on the table and when he saw me looking at it he offered me a piece.

'I thought we'd go ahead from there. It's only natural, between neighbours. I began to nibble a bit of chocolate and I had a squint at the book he was reading – something about Italy, with old pictures.

' "Don't you get bored, all alone here?" I asked him.

'I'm sure he wanted to. And I don't think I'm all that alarming. For a minute he was hesitating, I realized, and then, all at once, he stammered: "I have to go out. Someone's waiting for me . . ."'

'And that was all?'

'I'll say it was. The walls in this place aren't thick. You can hear every sound from one room to another. And he can't have got much sleep at night, if you see what I mean.

'But he never complained. You may have noticed on your way up that the toilets are at the far end of the corridor, above the stairs. One thing I can say for certain is that he didn't go to bed early, because I met him at least twice in the middle of the night, on his way to the toilet, still fully dressed.'

'Do you ever happen to glance at the house opposite?'

'The madwoman's house?'

'Why do you call her mad?'

'No special reason. I just think she looks mad. You know, one can see quite well from here. In the afternoon I've nothing to do, and sometimes I look out of the window. The people opposite don't often draw their curtains and when it gets dark those chandeliers look gorgeous. Huge glass chandeliers with dozens of lamps . . .

'Her room is right opposite this one. It's almost the only room where they do draw the curtains towards evening; but they pull them back in the morning, and she doesn't seem to realize that she can be seen from over here, walking about without a stitch on. Or perhaps she does it on purpose. Some women do carry on like that.

'She has two maids to wait on her, but she's just as likely to ring for the manservant when she's got nothing on.

'Some days her hairdresser comes in the middle of the afternoon – or later, on days when she's dolled up to the nines.

'She's not bad for her age, I will say that.'

'What age would you put her at?'

'Oh, forty-five-ish. But with women who take such care of themselves, you can't be sure.'

'Does she do much entertaining?'

'Sometimes there are two or three cars in the courtyard, not often more. It's usually she who goes out. Except for the gigolo, of course!'

'What gigolo?'

'I'm not suggesting he's a real gigolo. Though he's a bit on the young side for her, not a day over thirty. He's real handsome – tall, dark, and dressed like a tailor's dummy, and he drives a lovely car.'

'He often comes to see her?'

'I'm not always at the window, you know. I've my own job to do. Some days I begin about five in the afternoon, and that doesn't leave me much time to be staring into people's houses. Let's say he comes once or twice a week. Maybe three times.

'What I do know for sure is that he sometimes stays the night. Mostly I get up late, but on inspection days I have to be out at crack of dawn. One would think your chaps fix their hours on purpose. Well, two or three times the gigolo's car was still in the courtyard at nine in the morning.

'As for the other fellow . . .'

'Is there another?'

'I mean the old one – the one who pays.'

Maigret could not help smiling at Olga's interpretation of the facts.

'What's the matter? Have I said something silly?'

'Go ahead.'

'There's a real toff with grey hair who sometimes comes in a Rolls; he's got the handsomest chauffeur I've ever seen.'

'Does he ever spend the night there, too?'

'I don't think so. He never stays long. If I remember rightly, I've never seen him late in the evening. About five o'clock, that's more his style. For afternoon tea, I expect.'

She seemed delighted to show off her knowledge of the fact that, in a world remote from her own, there were people who took tea at five o'clock.

'I suppose you can't tell me why you're asking me all these questions?'

'No, I can't.'

'And I'm to keep my mouth shut?'

'I am most anxious that you should.'

'I'd better, for my own good – isn't that so? Don't be afraid. I'd heard about you from some of the other girls, but I thought you'd be older.'

She smiled at him, arching her body slightly beneath the bedclothes.

After a brief pause, she said softly:

'No?'

And he replied, smiling:

'No.'

At which she burst out laughing.

'Just like my neighbour!'

Then, suddenly serious:

'What's he done?'

Maigret was on the point of telling her the truth. It was a temptation. He knew he could rely on her. And he knew she would understand things better than Cajou, the examining magistrate, for instance. Perhaps some clue that hadn't occurred to him would strike her if he let her in on the story?

Later, if need be.

He turned to the door.

'Will you be coming back?'

'Very likely. What's the food like at the Petit Saint-Paul?'

'The owner does the cooking herself, and if you like *andouillettes* they're as good as any you'll find round here. But there are only paper tablecloths and the waitress is a bitch.'

It was noon when he walked into the Petit Saint-Paul, where

he began by telephoning to his wife to say he would not be home for lunch.

He was not forgetting Fernand and his gangsters, but he couldn't resist this business.

# Chapter Five

In fact he was giving himself a change, playing truant as it were, and he felt slightly guilty about it. But not too much so, because for one thing what Olga had said about the *andouillettes* was no exaggeration; for another thing the Beaujolais, though a little heavy, was very fruity; and lastly because, seated in a corner, at a table spread with rough paper instead of a cloth, he could ruminate at his ease.

The *patronne*, a short, stout woman with a bun of grey hair on top of her head, sometimes opened the kitchen door a crack and threw a rapid glance round the restaurant. She had a blue apron like the ones Maigret's mother used to wear long ago; the blue was still dark round the edges, but had faded in the middle, where it had been rubbed harder in the wash.

It was also true that the waitress, a tall, dark woman with a pasty complexion, looked sour and suspicious. From time to time she winced as though momentarily in pain, and the superintendent would have sworn she had just had a miscarriage.

The other customers included some workmen in their overalls, several Algerians, and a newspaper-woman in man's jacket and peaked cap.

What would be the use of showing a photo of Cuendet to the waitress or to the heavily moustached *patron* who was attending to the wine? From the table where Maigret was sitting, and which had no doubt been his as well, the Swiss – provided he wiped the steamy window-pane every three minutes – could have kept an eye on the street and on the house that interested him.

He had certainly not confided in anybody. He must have been taken, as he was everywhere, for just a quiet little man; and in a sense this was true.

In his own way, Cuendet was a craftsman; and because Maigret was thinking at the same time about the fellows in the Rue La Fayette – that was what he called ruminating – he found the man slightly old-fashioned – like this restaurant, which would soon make way for a spick-and-span self-service counter.

Maigret had known other solitary workers, such as the famous Commodore, with his monocle and the red carnation in his button-hole, who used to stay in the most fashionable hotels – a faultlessly attired, dignified, white-haired figure – and was never once caught red-handed.

The Commodore had never seen the inside of a prison, and no one knew how he had met his end. Had he retired to the country with a change of identity, or spent his declining years basking in the sunshine of an island in the South Seas? Had he been murdered by some tough with an eye to his savings?

At that time, too, there had been organized gangs; but their methods of work were not the same as nowadays, and above all they were differently composed.

Twenty years ago, for instance, in a matter like the Rue La Fayette affair, Maigret would have known at once where to look – the exact district and almost the exact tavern frequented by the bad lots. In those days they could scarcely read or write, and their way of life was written all over their faces.

Nowadays they were skilled technicians. This hold-up in the Rue La Fayette like its forerunners had been meticulously planned and the capture of one of the men involved was due to the most improbable accident – the presence in the crowd of a police constable who in defiance of regulations was armed although not on duty, and who had lost his head and fired, at the risk of hitting some inoffensive member of the crowd.

Even Cuendet had brought himself up to date, that was true. Maigret called to mind a remark made by the woman in the next room at the hotel. She had referred to people who took afternoon tea at five o'clock. To her, they belonged to a world of their own. To Maigret likewise. But Cuendet had been at pains to make a careful study of such people's habits and customs.

He broke no window-panes, used no jemmy, did no damage.

Out in the street, people were walking quickly, their hands in their pockets, their faces stiff with cold, everyone brooding over his own problems and worries, everyone with his personal drama, everyone compelled to some form of activity.

'My bill, please.'

The waitress wrote down the items in pencil on the paper tablecloth, her lips moving and her eyes turning now and then to the slate on which the prices of the various dishes were marked.

Maigret went back to the office on foot. No sooner was he seated at his desk, with his files and his pipes arrayed in front of him, than the door opened and Lucas appeared. They both opened their mouths at the same time. The superintendent was the first to speak.

'Someone should be sent to take over from Fumel, at the Hôtel Lambert in the Rue Neuve Saint-Pierre.'

Not a member of what might be called his personal team, but a man like Lourtie, for instance, or Lesueur. Neither of these was free, and it was Baron who left the Quai des Orfèvres a little later, suitably briefed.

'And you? What did you want to tell me?'

'There's been a new development. Inspector Nicolas may have put his finger on something.'

'Is he here?'

'Yes – waiting to see you.'

'Send him in.'

Nicolas was an inconspicuous kind of man, and because of that fact he had been sent to prowl round Fontenay-aux-Roses. His job was to get into casual conversation with the Raisons' neighbours, the shopkeepers they dealt with, and the mechanics at the garage where the wounded gangster kept his car.

'I can't say yet if this will lead us anywhere, chief, but I rather think we may have got hold of something. Yesterday evening I discovered that Raison and his wife were on visiting terms with another couple in the same block of flats. In fact they were great friends. They sometimes watched television together in the evening. When they went to the cinema, one of the wives would stay behind to look after the other family's children as well as her own.

'The name of this couple is Lussac. They're younger than the Raisons. René Lussac is only thirty-one and his wife is two or three years less than that. She's very pretty and they have a little boy of two and a half.

'Acting on your instructions, I therefore began to watch René Lussac, who travels for a firm of musical-instrument makers. Like Raison, he has a car – a Floride.

'Yesterday evening I followed him when he left home after dinner. I had the use of an old car. He had no idea I was trailing him, or he could easily have shaken me off.

'He went to a café at the Porte de Versailles, the Café des Amis – a quiet place, popular with the local tradesmen, who come there for a game of cards.

'Two men were waiting for him, and they began to play *belote*, like people who are in the habit of meeting round the same table.

'It struck me as a bit peculiar. Lussac has never lived anywhere near the Porte de Versailles. I wondered why he came such a long way to play cards in such an unattractive joint.'

'You were inside the café?'

'Yes. I felt certain he hadn't spotted me at Fontenay-aux-Roses, so I was running no risk by showing myself. He took no notice of me. The three of them were playing in quite a natural way, but they looked at the time rather often.

'At precisely half-past nine Lussac went to the cashdesk and bought a counter for the automatic telephone. He shut himself up in the phone-box, where he remained for about ten minutes. I could see him through the glass. It wasn't a Paris call, because after lifting off the receiver he only said a few words and then hung up. He waited in the booth, and after a few minutes the telephone rang. In other words the call had been put through by tolls or long-distance.

'When he came back to his table he was looking worried. He said something to the others and then glanced round suspiciously and signed to them to go on with the game.'

'What did the other two look like?'

'I went out before they left, and waited in my car. I thought there was no point in following Lussac, who would no doubt be going back to Fontenay-aux-Roses. So I chose one of the others, at random. They both had cars. The one who looked to be the older of the two was the first to drive off, and I followed him to a garage in the Rue La Boétie. He left his car there and walked to a house in the Rue de Ponthieu, parallel with the Champs-Élysées, where he had a one-roomed furnished flat.

'His name is Georges Macagne. I got the hotel squad to look into that this morning. Then I went up and found his file. He's had two sentences for car thefts and one for assault.'

This was perhaps the long-awaited gleam of light.

'I thought it would be better not to question the café proprietors.'

'Quite right. I'll ask the examining magistrate for a warrant, and you must take it to the telephone exchange and get them to find out who René Lussac rang up last night. They won't do anything without a written order.'

The inspector was scarcely out of his office before Maigret had rung up the Hôpital Beaujon. He had some difficulty in getting hold of the man who was on duty outside Raison's door.

'How is he now?'

'I was just waiting a few minutes before ringing you. Someone went to fetch his wife. She's just arrived. I can hear her crying in his room. Half a minute. The matron has just come out. Will you hold on?'

Maigret could still hear the muffled sounds typical of a hospital corridor.

'Hello? It's what I thought. He's dead.'

'He didn't say anything?'

'He never even recovered consciousness. His wife is lying on her face on the floor, sobbing.'

'Did she notice you?'

'I'm sure she didn't, not in the state she's in.'

'She came by taxi?'

'I don't know.'

'Go down to the main entrance and wait. Follow her when she leaves, on the off-chance that she may feel like getting in touch with somebody, or making a telephone call.'

'Okay, chief.'

Perhaps the case might be practically over, and a telephone call would at last lead them to Fernand. It would be quite consistent for him to be lying low somewhere in the country, near Paris, probably in some inn kept by a retired prostitute or an ex-gangster.

If the telephone gave no results they could always make the round of such places, but that might take a long time, and Fernand, the brains of the gang, might very well be in the habit of changing his hide-out every day.

Maigret rang up the examining magistrate in charge of the investigation, told him what had happened, promised him a report, and then settled down to write it at once, for the magistrate wanted to speak to the public prosecutor that night.

Maigret mentioned, among other things, that the car used for the hold-up had been found near the Porte d'Italie. As was to be expected, it was a stolen car, and naturally it had yielded no clues whatsoever, let alone any interesting fingerprints.

He was hard at work when old Joseph, the office messenger, came in to say that the director of the judicial police would like to see him in his office. For a moment Maigret thought it was about the Cuendet business – that in some mysterious way his chief had got wind of his activities – and he expected a rap over the knuckles.

In point of fact it was about a new case altogether – the disappearance, three days previously, of the daughter of a prominent man. She was a girl of seventeen, and it had been discovered that she was surreptitiously attending a drama school and had done crowd work in several films that were not yet released.

'Her parents want to keep it out of the papers. There's every likelihood that she went off of her own accord . . .'

He put Lapointe on this affair and returned to his report while the sky outside the windows grew darker and darker.

At five o'clock he knocked on the door of the office belonging to his colleague, the head of General Information, a man with the bearing of a cavalry officer. Here there was no rush, no bustling to and fro, as there was with the crime squad. The walls were lined with green files and the lock on the door was as complicated as that of a strongroom.

'Tell me, Danet, do you happen to know a man called Wilton?'

'Why do you ask?'

'It's still rather vague. Someone's been talking to me about him and I'd like to have a few more particulars.'

'Is he mixed up in some trouble?'

'I don't think so.'

'It's Stuart Wilton you mean?'

'Yes.'

So Danet did know the man, as he knew every foreigner of any standing who lived in Paris or came there for long visits. Among the green files there might even be one bearing Wilton's name; but the head of General Information made no move to produce it.

'He's a very important man.'

'I know. And very wealthy, so I'm told.'

'Very wealthy, yes, and a good friend of France. In fact he chooses to live in this country for the greater part of the year.'

'Why?'

'For one thing because he likes the life.'

'And then?'

'Perhaps because he feels freer here than across the Channel. What puzzles me is your coming to ask me questions, because I don't see any possible connection between Stuart Wilton and your department.'

'There isn't any as yet.'

'Is it because of a woman that you're on to him?'

'One can't even say I am on to him. There is certainly a woman who . . .'

'Which one?'

'He's been married several times, hasn't he?'

'Three times. And no doubt he will marry again one of these days, although he's getting on for seventy.'

'He takes a great interest in women?'

'He does.'

Danet's replies came reluctantly, as though Maigret were trespassing on his own private preserves.

'In others besides those he marries, I take it?'

'Naturally.'

'How do things stand between him and his wife?'

'You mean the French one?'

'Yes, Florence; the one who – so I'm told – used to belong to a troupe of dancers.'

'He has remained on excellent terms with her – and with his two previous wives, for that matter. The first was the daughter of a rich English brewer, and she gave him a son. She married again and now lives in the Bahamas.

'The second was a young actress. He had no children by her and left her after only two or three years; he has lent her a villa on the Riviera and she lives quietly down there.'

'And to Florence he's given a house in Paris,' Maigret muttered.

Danet frowned uneasily.

'She's the one you're interested in?'

'I don't know yet.'

'It's not as though she goes in for publicity. But of course I've never had occasion to study Wilton from that angle. I only know what is common knowledge in a certain circle in Paris.

'Yes, Florence lives in a house that used to belong to her ex-husband . . .'

'In the Rue Neuve Saint-Pierre . . .'

'Correct. But I'm not sure the house is hers. As I said, each time Wilton has been divorced he has remained on excellent terms with his last wife. He allows them to keep their jewellery and furs; but I doubt if he would make one of them a present of a house such as that.'

'What about his son?'

'He spends part of his time in Paris, too, but not so much as his father. He does a lot of skiing in Switzerland and Austria, goes in for motor racing and yacht racing on the Riviera, in England and in Italy, plays polo . . .'

'In other words, no professional activity?'

'Definitely none.'

'Married?'

'He was, for a year, to a model; then he divorced her. Listen, Maigret, I don't want to have a battle of wits with you. I don't know what you're after, or what's at the back of your mind. All I ask is that you'll do nothing without telling me. I meant what I said about Stuart Wilton being a good friend of France, and it's not for nothing that he's a Commander of the Legion of Honour.

'He has enormous interests in this country and he's a man to be treated with tact.

'His private life is none of our business, unless he has committed some serious breach of the law, and that would surprise me.

'He's a man for the women. To be quite frank, I shouldn't be surprised to learn that he has some kind of hidden kink. But I'd just as soon not know what it is.

'As for the son and his divorce, I may as well tell you what was rumoured at the time, because you'll find out in any case.

'Lida, the model young Wilton married, was an exceptionally beautiful girl – of Hungarian origin, if I'm not mistaken . . . Stuart Wilton was against the marriage. His son ignored his objections and they say he discovered, one fine day, that his wife was his father's mistress.

'There was no scandal. In those circles there seldom is; people settle things quietly, like men of the world.

'So young Wilton got a divorce.'

'And Lida?'

'All this happened about three years ago. Since then her photo has often appeared in the papers, because she has had affairs with several internationally celebrated men, and if I'm not mistaken she's now living in Rome with an Italian prince. Is that what you wanted to hear about?'

'I don't know.'

This was true. Maigret felt tempted to lay his cards on the

table and tell his colleague the whole story. But their points of view were too far apart.

To put it in terms of what Olga had said that morning, Superintendent Danet probably took afternoon tea now and then; whereas Maigret had lunched at a bistro with paper tablecloths, in the company of workmen and Algerians.

'I'll come and see you again when I have some idea. By the way, is Stuart Wilton in Paris at the moment?'

'Unless he's on the Riviera. I can find out. It would be better for me to do it myself.'

'And his son?'

'He lives in the residential part of the Hôtel George V; rents a flat there by the year.'

'Thank you, Danet.'

'Be careful, Maigret!'

'I promise!'

The superintendent had no intention of ringing Stuart Wilton's door-bell and beginning to ask him questions. And at the George V he would get no more than politely evasive answers.

Cajou, the examining magistrate, had known what he was about when he made that statement to the Press, saying that the Bois de Boulogne business was connected with some vendetta in the underworld. It implied that there was no need to get excited, or try to find out too much.

There are some crimes that cause a public sensation. It may be for some quite adventitious reason – the identity of the victim, the manner of the crime, or the place where it was committed.

For instance, if Cuendet had been murdered in a Champs-Élysées nightclub he would have hit the front-page headlines.

As it was, his death had passed almost unnoticed, with nothing to capture the attention of people reading their morning paper in the Métro. An ex-convict who had never committed any sensational crime and who could just as easily have been fished up somewhere along the Seine.

Yet Cuendet interested Maigret more than Fernand and his gang, although he had no right to take an official hand in the case.

For the gangsters of the Rue La Fayette, the whole police force was to stand by for action. Whereas Fumel, with no car at his disposal and no assurance that if he ventured to take a taxi the fare would be refunded to him, had sole responsibility for the Cuendet investigation.

He must have gone to the Rue Mouffetard, searched Justine's flat and asked her questions to which she would have replied precisely as she chose.

All the same, Maigret telephoned from his office to the Medico-Legal Institute. Instead of asking for Doctor Lamalle or one of his assistants, he decided to speak to a laboratory attendent he had known for a long time and for whom he had once done a good turn.

'Tell me, François, were you at the post-mortem on Honoré Cuendet, the Bois de Boulogne chap?'

'Yes, I was. Haven't you had the report?'

'I'm not in charge of the case; but I'd like to know, all the same.'

'I understand. Well, Doctor Lamalle thinks this customer had been hit about ten times. To begin with he was struck from behind, so violently that his skull was smashed in and death must have been instantaneous. Doctor Lamalle's a very nice man, you know. We still miss dear old Doctor Paul, of course; but everyone likes Lamalle already.'

'What about the other blows?'

'They were delivered on the man's face when he was already lying on his back.'

'What type of weapon do they think was used?'

'They discussed that for a long time and even made some

experiments. It seems it wasn't a knife, or a monkey-wrench, or any of the usual things. Not a jemmy or a knuckle-duster, either. I overheard them saying that the object used must have had several projections, and was heavy and bulky.'

'A statue?'

'That's the suggestion they made in their report.'

'Were they able to fix the approximate time of death?'

'According to them it was about two in the morning. Between half-past one and three, but nearer two o'clock.'

'Did he bleed a lot?'

'Not only that, but some of his brains came out. There were still traces in his hair.'

'The contents of the stomach were analysed?'

'Guess what it contained! Chocolate, not yet digested. There was some alcohol too; not much, and it was only just beginning to enter the blood-stream.'

'Thank you, François. Unless you're asked, don't say I rang up.'

'Better not for my own sake, too.'

Fumel telephoned the superintendent a little later.

'I called to see the old woman, chief, and she went with me to the Medico-Legal Institute. It's him, right enough.'

'How did it go?'

'She was less upset than I'd feared. When I offered to take her home she refused, and went off all alone to the Métro station.'

'You searched the flat?'

'I found nothing except books and magazines.'

'No photographs?'

'Only a bad photo of the father in Swiss uniform, and a cabinet photograph of Honoré as a baby.'

'No notes? You went through the books?'

'Nothing. The man didn't write, and received no letters. Nor did his mother, needless to say.'

'There's one trail you might follow up, provided you're very cautious. A certain Stuart Wilton lives in the Rue de Long-champ, where he owns a big house – I don't know the number. He has a Rolls-Royce and a chauffeur. They must occasionally leave the car out in the street or put it into a garage. Try to see if there isn't a wild-cat rug inside.

'Wilton's son lives at the George V and has a car too.'

'I understand, chief.'

'That's not all. It would be interesting to get hold of photos of them both.'

'I know a photographer who works in the Champs-Élysées.'

'Good luck to you!'

Maigret spent half an hour signing forms, and when he left the office he set out on foot for the Saint-Paul district, instead of making for his usual bus.

It was as cold as ever and as dark; the city lights seemed unusually bright, and the passers-by were seen in blacker silhouette, as though all half-tones had been eliminated.

As he turned the corner of the Rue Saint-Paul, a voice out of the darkness said:

'Well, superintendent?'

It was Olga, in a rabbit-fur coat, standing in a doorway. This gave him the idea of asking her for some information he had been meaning to seek elsewhere – particularly as she was the person most likely to be able to supply it.

'Tell me, when you need a drink or want to warm yourself after midnight, what's open round here?'

'Chez Léon.'

'That's a bar?'

'Yes. In the Rue Saint-Antoine, just opposite the Métro.'

'Did you ever meet your neighbour there?'

'The Swiss? No, not at night. Once or twice in the afternoon.'

'Drinking?'

'White wine.'

'Thank you.'

This time it was she who, as she tramped off, called out:

'Good luck to you!'

He had a photo of Cuendet in his pocket, and going into the steamy bar he ordered a glass of brandy – regretting it when he saw there were six or seven stars on the bottle.

'Do you know this man?'

The *patron* wiped his hands on his apron before taking hold of the photograph, which he then studied thoughtfully.

'What's he done?' he inquired cautiously.

'He's dead.'

'How? Suicide?'

'What makes you suppose that?'

'I don't know . . . I didn't see him often . . . Three or four times . . . He never talked to anyone . . . The last evening . . .'

'When was that?'

'I couldn't tell you for certain . . . Thursday or Friday of last week . . . Maybe Saturday . . . The other times he'd come for a quick one at the bar in the afternoon, like a man who's thirsty . . .'

'Only one glass?'

'Two, perhaps . . . Not more . . . He wasn't what you'd call a drinker . . . I can recognize them at first glance.'

'What time was it, the last evening?'

'After midnight . . . Wait a minute . . . My wife had gone upstairs . . . So it must have been between half-past twelve and one o'clock . . .'

'How do you happen to remember?'

'Well, for one thing, at night we get hardly anybody except the regulars; sometimes a taxi-driver on the crawl, or a couple of police having a glass on the sly . . . I remember there was one couple at the corner table, talking in whispers . . . Otherwise the place was empty. I was busy with the coffee percolator. I didn't hear any footsteps. And when I turned round, there he was, leaning on the bar. It gave me quite a turn.'

'That's why you remember it?'

'And for another reason, because he asked me if I had any real kirsch, not the fancy stuff . . . We don't get many orders for that. I took a bottle from the back row – that one there, with the German words on the label – and he seemed pleased. He said:

' "That's the real thing." '

'He took the time to warm the glass in his hand, and drank slowly, looking at the clock. I realized he was wondering whether to ask for another, and when I held out the bottle he didn't say no.

'He wasn't drinking for the sake of drinking, but because he liked kirsch.'

'He didn't speak to anybody?'

'Only to me.'

'The people in the corner took no notice of him?'

'They were a pair of lovers. I know them. They come here twice a week and sit whispering for hours, gazing into each other's eyes.'

'They left soon after he did?'

'Indeed they did not.'

'You didn't notice anyone who might have been watching him from outside?'

The man shrugged his shoulders as though he felt insulted.

'I've been in this place for fifteen years . . .' he sighed.

The implication being that nothing unusual could escape his notice.

A little later on, Maigret walked into the Hôtel Lambert, and this time it was the proprietress who was in the office. She was younger and more attractive than the superintendent would have expected after seeing her husband.

'You've come about number 33, haven't you? The gentleman's up there now.'

'Thank you.'

On the way up he had to flatten himself against the wall to make way for a couple coming down. The woman was drenched in scent and the man turned his head aside, looking sheepish.

The room was in darkness. Baron was sitting in the armchair, which he had drawn up to the window. He must have got through a whole packet of cigarettes, for the atmosphere was suffocating.

'Anything happened?'

'She went out half an hour ago. Before that a woman came to see her, carrying a big cardboard box – a seamstress or a dressmaker, I suppose. They went into the bedroom together and all I could see was their shadows going to and fro and then keeping quite still, with one of them kneeling down, as though a dress was being tried on.'

There were no lights on the ground floor except in the hall. The stairs were lit as far as the second floor, and two lamps were still burning in the drawing-room, on the left; but not the big chandelier.

To the right was the boudoir, where a lace-capped maid in black dress and white apron was tidying up.

'The kitchen and dining-room must be at the back. The way these people go on, one wonders what they do all day. I counted at least three servants going to and fro with no sign of what they were up to. There've been no visitors except the dressmaker. She came by taxi and left on foot, without her cardboard box. An errand-boy arrived on a box-tricycle and delivered some parcels. The manservant came out and took them from him. Do I carry on?'

'Are you hungry?'

'Beginning to be, but I can wait.'

'Get along now.'

'Shouldn't I stay till someone else takes over?'

Maigret shrugged. What was the use?

He locked the door and put the key in his pocket. Downstairs, he said to the proprietress:

'Don't let number 33 till you hear from me. Nobody is to go in there; you understand?'

In the street he caught sight of Olga approaching from a distance, arm in arm with a man, and he felt glad for her.

# Chapter Six

He sat down to dinner with no suspicion that a telephone call was soon to summon him from the rather cloying tranquillity of his flat, that a considerable number of people who were at present making plans for the evening were destined to spend the night otherwise than they had intended, or that every window in the building in the Quai des Orfèvres would be lit up until morning, as only happened on nights when there was a great to-do.

It was a very pleasant dinner, with a cosy sense of tacit understanding between Maigret and his wife. He told her about having *andouillettes* for lunch at the bistro in the Saint-Antoine district. They had often gone together to such places, which were more numerous in the old days, typical of Paris. There used to be one in nearly every street and they were known as lorry-drivers' restaurants.

'You know, the real reason one ate so well there was that they were all owned by people who'd come straight from their native provinces – Auvergne, Brittany, Normandy, Burgundy – and who not only kept up the traditions they'd brought with them, but were in constant touch with home and sent to the country for hams and terrines and sausages, sometimes even for bread . . .'

This reminded him of Cuendet and his mother, who had brought with them to the Rue Mouffetard the slow speech of the Vaudois Swiss, with a kind of static placidity that had a suggestion of laziness about it.

'Any news of the old woman?'

Madame Maigret had read his thoughts in his face.

'You forget that officially, for the moment, I'm only dealing with the hold-ups. They're more serious, they are – because they're a threat to the banks and insurance companies, to big business. The gangsters have modernized their methods quicker than we have.'

He said this with a shade of fleeting melancholy. Or rather, of regret for the past. His wife recognized it as such, and knew it never lasted long.

At such moments, incidentally, he was less alarmed by the thought of his retirement, only two years ahead. The world was changing, Paris was changing, everything was changing – men and methods alike. If it weren't for retirement, though at times it seemed such a bogey, wouldn't he begin to feel lost in a world he no longer understood?

And all the same he was eating with relish, leisurely.

'He was a funny fellow! He had no reason to anticipate what's happened to him, and yet when I hinted to his mother that I was anxious about her future, she only said calmly:

'"*I'm sure he won't leave me without a penny . . .*"'

If that were so, how had Cuendet managed it? What scheme had he finally worked out in his big bullet-head?

And then, just as Maigret was beginning his dessert, the telephone rang.

'Would you like me to answer?'

But he was already on his feet, napkin in hand.

It was Janvier, calling from the Quai des Orfèvres.

'There's some news that may be important, chief. Inspector Nicolas has just rung me. They've traced the call René Lussac made from the café at the Porte de Versailles.

'It was to a number just outside Corbeil, a villa on the Seine, which belongs to somebody you know – Rosalie Bourdon.'

*La belle Rosalie!*'

'Yes. I rang the police patrol at Corbeil. They say she's at home.'

This, too, was someone who had frequently spent hours on end in Maigret's office. She was getting on for fifty now, but she was still an appetizing creature – plump, florid, and with a flow of vivid, spicy language.

She had begun her career very young, on a stretch of pavement near the Place des Ternes, and at the age of twenty-five she was running an establishment whose clients included some of the most distinguished men in Paris.

Later she had moved to the Rue Notre-Dame de Lorette and opened a nightclub of a specialized character, which went by the name of La Cravache.

Her last lover, the great love of her life, had been a certain Pierre Sabatini, a member of the Corsican gang, who had been sentenced to twenty years' hard labour for shooting down two members of the Marseilles gang in a bar in the Rue de Douai.

Sabatini would be at Saint-Martin-de-Ré for quite a few years yet. Rosalie had taken a deeply emotional line at the trial, and after her lover was sentenced she had moved heaven and earth for permission to marry him.

The papers had been full of it at the time. She had declared that she was expecting a child. Some people suspected that she had got herself pregnant by the first comer, in the hope of bringing off the marriage.

In any case, once the Ministry had refused to issue a permit there had been no further suggestion of maternity, and Rosalie had withdrawn from the public eye to her villa near Corbeil, whence she wrote and sent parcels to the prisoner at frequent intervals. She made a trip to the Ile de Ré every month, and the authorities down there kept a close eye on her, fearing that she was plotting her lover's escape.

And Fernand had been Sabatini's cell-mate at Saint-Martin. Janvier went on:

'I've asked the people at Corbeil to set a watch on the villa. Several men are stationed round it now.'

'And Nicolas?'

'He asked me to tell you he was going back to the Porte de Versailles. What he saw yesterday gave him the impression that Lussac and his two friends are meeting there every evening. He wanted to be settled in the café before them, so as to reduce the risk of attracting their attention.'

'Is Lucas still in the office?'

'He's just back.'

'Tell him to keep a few men in reserve tonight. I'll ring you again in a few minutes.'

He rang up the Public Prosecutor's office, but there was only a subordinate on duty.

'I'd like to speak to Monsieur Dupont d'Hastier himself.'

'He's not here.'

'I know. But I need to speak to him urgently. It's about the latest hold-up, and probably about Fernand.'

'I'll try to get in touch with him. Are you at the Quai?'

'No, at home.'

He gave his telephone number, and then things began to happen in rapid succession. He had scarcely finished his dessert when the telephone rang again. It was the Public Prosecutor.

'They tell me you've arrested Fernand?'

'Not yet, sir, but we may have a chance of arresting him tonight.'

He explained the situation in a few rapid sentences.

'Meet me in my office in a quarter of an hour. I'm dining with friends, but I shall be leaving at once. You've got in touch with Corbeil?'

Madame Maigret made him some strong coffee and brought out the bottle of framboise from the sideboard cupboard.

'Take care not to catch cold. Do you suppose you'll be going to Corbeil?'

'I shall be surprised if they give me the chance.'

He was not mistaken. At the Palais de Justice, in one of the big offices in the public prosecutor's department, he found the Prosecutor himself, Monsieur Dupont d'Hastier, in a dinner-jacket, and with him Monsieur Legaille, the examining magistrate in charge of the inquiry into hold-ups, and Superintendent Buffet, an old colleague of his own from the 'other branch', the Sûreté Nationale.

Buffet was taller, broader and more thick-set than Maigret, with a red face and sleepy-looking eyes – despite which he was one of the most efficient men in the force.

'Sit down, Maigret, and tell us exactly where you've got to.'

Before leaving home he had made another call to Janvier.

'I'm expecting news to come through here, any minute now. One thing I can tell you already – Rosalie Bourdon's had a man in her house at Corbeil for the last few days.'

'Have our men seen him?' asked Buffet; for all his massive body he had a tiny voice, almost like a girl's.

'Not yet, but some of the neighbours have told them about him, and what they said tallies pretty well with the description of Fernand.'

'Are they surrounding the house?'

'Yes – at some distance, so as not to give the alarm.'

'There's more than one way out?'

'Yes, of course. But there are other developments as well. As I told the prosecutor just now on the telephone, Lussac was friendly with Joseph Raison, the gangster who was killed in the Rue La Fayette, they both lived in the same block of flats at Fontenay-aux-Roses. And Lussac, with at least two friends, is going regularly to a café at the Porte de Versailles, the Café des Amis.

'They were there yesterday evening, playing cards, and at half-past nine Lussac went into the telephone-box and rang up Corbeil.

'So that seems to be how the three men keep in touch with their leader. I'm expecting a call from one minute to the next.

'Now if – as we shall soon know – they are meeting at the same place this evening, we shall have a decision to make.'

In the old days he would have made the decision himself, and this kind of council of war in the public prosecutor's office would never have been held. In fact it would have been unthinkable, except in a case with political implications.

'A witness has declared that at the time of the hold-up Fernand was sitting in a café exactly opposite the spot where the cashier was attacked and where his accomplices – all but one – jumped into their car.

'Those men went off with the briefcase containing the money.

'It's not likely that Fernand has been able to meet them since then, particularly in view of the accident that took place.

'If it is he who is hiding in Rosalie's house, he must have gone there that same evening, and every evening he issues his instructions by telephone to the Café des Amis . . .'

Buffet was listening sleepily. Maigret knew that his colleague was considering the matter from the same angle as himself, anticipating the same possibilities and dangers. It was only for the gentlemen of the public prosecutor's department that he was going into all these details.

'Sooner or later, one of the accomplices will be told to bring all or part of the loot to Fernand. If that happens, of course, we shall have conclusive evidence. But there may be several days to wait. Meanwhile, it's on the cards that Fernand will look for another hide-out, and even with a watch on the villa he might easily give us the slip.

'On the other hand, if there is a meeting at the Café des Amis this evening, as there was yesterday, we shall have a chance to arrest all three men and to get our hands on Fernand at Corbeil at the same time.'

The telephone rang. The clerk handed the receiver to Maigret.

'It's for you.'

It was Janvier, acting as a kind of go-between.

'They are there, chief. What have you decided?'

'I'll tell you in a few minutes. Send one of our men, and a woman welfare officer, to Fontenay-aux-Roses. Tell him to ring you up as soon as he gets there.'

'Right.'

Maigret rang off.

'What is your decision, gentlemen?'

'To run no risk,' replied the public prosecutor. 'We shall get our evidence in the end, shall we not?'

'They will engage the best solicitors and refuse to give anything away, and they've no doubt provided themselves with first-class alibis.'

'Still, if we don't arrest them tonight we may never get another chance.'

'I'll take care of Corbeil,' Buffet announced.

It was not for Maigret to protest. That end was outside his sector.

'Do you think they'll shoot?' asked the examining magistrate.

'Almost certainly, if they have the opportunity; but we'll try not to leave the decision to them.'

A few minutes later, Maigret and his stout colleague moved from one world to another by going through the inconspicuous door that divided the Palais de Justice from the offices of the Judicial Police.

Here the atmosphere was already tense with anticipation.

'We'd better wait before attacking the villa, in case they make a telephone call at half-past nine.'

'Right you are. But I'd rather get there ahead of time, so as to have everything ready. I'll ring up to find out how you stand.'

In the dark, cold courtyard a radio car was already waiting, with its engine warming up, and a van loaded with police stood beside it. The superintendent of police for the 16th *arrondissement* must by now be somewhere close to the Café des Amis, with all the men he could muster.

Peaceful shopkeepers were sitting in the café, discussing business or playing cards, with no suspicion of what was going on; and nobody noticed Inspector Nicolas, who was deep in his newspaper.

He had just telephoned his laconic report:

'It's done.'

This meant that the three men were there, as they had been the previous day – René Lussac glancing at the clock now and then, no doubt to make sure he would not be late for his call to Corbeil at nine-thirty.

Spread out round the house at Corbeil, where two ground-floor windows were lit up, men were standing motionless in the darkness, among the ice-coated puddles.

The telephone exchange had been warned and was waiting. At nine thirty-five it reported:

'We have just been asked to ring Corbeil.'

And an inspector at the listening-post recorded the ensuing conversation.

'Everything okay?' asked Lussac.

It was not a man who answered, it was Rosalie.

'Okay. Nothing new.'

'Jules is getting impatient.'

'Why?'

'He wants to go off on a trip.'

'Hold on a minute.'

She must have gone to consult somebody. Soon she was back:

'He says you must wait a bit longer.'

'Why?'

'Just because.'

'They're beginning to look at us suspiciously in this place.'

'Wait a minute.'

Another silence, and then:

'There'll be some news tomorrow, for sure.'

Buffet rang up from Corbeil.

'Okay?'

'Yes. Lussac made his call. It was the woman who answered, but there's someone there with her. It seems that one of the gang, a fellow called Jules, is getting impatient.'

'So we can go ahead?'

'At ten-fifteen.'

The two operations must be synchronized, so that if by some miracle one of the men escaped the raid on the café, he would not be able to raise the alarm at Corbeil.

'At ten-fifteen.'

Maigret gave Janvier his final instructions.

'When you get the call from Fontenay-aux-Roses, tell 'em to arrest Madame Lussac, with or without a warrant, and bring her here, leaving the welfare officer to look after the child.'

'And Madame Raison?'

'No, not her. Not at present.'

Maigret climbed into the radio car. The police van had already left. At the Porte de Versailles a few pedestrians raised their eyebrows as they noticed the air of unusual activity, with men keeping close to houses and talking in low voices, and others disappearing into dark corners as though by magic.

Maigret got hold of the local superintendent and settled with him how things should be done.

Here again, they had the choice between two alternatives. They could wait for the three card-players – whom they could see from a distance, through the café windows – to emerge and go to their respective cars, which were parked near by, as on the previous evening.

This seemed to be the easiest course. But it was the most risky, for, once outside, the men would have complete freedom of movement, and perhaps time to use their guns. And might not one of them manage, during the scuffle, to jump into his car and escape?

'Is there another way out of the place?'

'There's a door into the yard, but the walls are high and the only way to the street is the corridor through the house.'

It took them less than a quarter of an hour to place their men, without attracting any attention in the Café des Amis.

Several men who might pass for tenants of the upstairs flats went into the house, and some of them stood about the yard.

Three others – hearty types and slightly tipsy – pushed into the café and sat down at the table next to the card-players.

Maigret glanced at his watch now and then, like a military commander waiting for zero hour, and at fourteen minutes past ten he went into the café, alone.

His neck was swathed in his knitted muffler and he kept his right hand in his overcoat pocket.

He had only two yards to go, and the gangsters had not even time to jump to their feet. Standing close beside them, he said in an undertone: 'Don't move. You are surrounded. Keep your hands on the table.'

Inspector Nicolas had joined him by now.

'Put the handcuffs on them. You others, too.'

One of the men managed to upset the table with a sudden jerk, and they heard the crash of broken glass but two inspectors already had him by the wrists.

'Outside . . .'

Maigret looked round at the customers.

'Don't be alarmed, ladies and gentlemen; that was just a police operation.'

Fifteen minutes later the police van deposited the three men at the Quai des Orfèvres, where they were taken to separate offices.

A call came through from Corbeil: it was the burly Buffet, inquiring in his piping voice:

'Maigret? We're through.'

'No hitch?'

'He managed to shoot, all the same, and one of my fellows has a bullet in the shoulder.'

'What about the woman?'

'My face is covered with scratches. I'll bring you the pair of 'em as soon as I've seen to the formalities.'

The telephone never stopped ringing. This time it was the Public Prosecutor.

'Yes, sir. We've got them all. No, I've not asked them a single question. I've put them into separate offices and now I'm waiting for the man and woman Buffet is bringing me from Corbeil.'

'Be careful. Don't forget they'll make out that the police have third-degreed them.'

'I know.'

'And that they have a perfect right to refuse to say a word unless there is a solicitor present.'

'Yes, sir . . .'

In any case Maigret did not intend to question them right away, thinking it better to leave them to stew in their juice, separately. He was waiting for Madame Lussac.

She did not arrive until eleven o'clock, for she was in bed when the inspector got to the flat, and it had taken her some time to get dressed and explain to the woman welfare officer what might need to be done for her little boy.

She was a thin, dark-haired, rather pretty woman of not more than twenty-five or so. Her face was pale and pinched. She said nothing, not bothering to feign indignation.

Maigret asked her to sit down facing him, while Janvier

installed himself at the end of the desk with paper and pencil.

'Your husband's name is René Lussac and he is a commercial traveller by profession?'

'Yes, monsieur.'

'He is thirty-one years of age. How long have you been married?'

'Four years.'

'What was your maiden name?'

'Jacqueline Beaudet.'

'Born in Paris?'

'No, Orléans. I came to live in Paris with an aunt, when I was sixteen.'

'What does your aunt do?'

'She's a midwife. She lives in the Rue Notre-Dame de Lorette.'

'Where did you meet René Lussac?'

'In a record and musical instrument shop where I was working as an assistant. Where is he, superintendent? Tell me what's happened to him. Ever since Joseph . . .'

'You mean Joseph Raison?'

'Yes. Joseph and his wife were friends of ours. We live in the same block of flats.'

'Did the two men often go out together?'

'Sometimes. Not often. Ever since Joseph died . . .'

'You have been afraid the same kind of accident might happen to your husband – isn't that so?'

'Where is he? Has he disappeared?'

'No. He's here.'

'Alive?'

'Yes.'

'Wounded?'

'He might well have been, but he isn't.'

'Can I see him?'

'Not just yet.'

'Why not?'

She added with a bitter smile:

'Silly of me to ask you that! I can guess what you want, why you're questioning me. You're thinking it will be easier to make a woman talk than a man, isn't that it?'

'Fernand has been arrested.'

'Who's he?'

'Do you really not know?'

She looked him straight in the eyes.

'No. My husband has never mentioned him to me. All I know is that someone gives orders.'

She had produced a handkerchief from her handbag, as a concession to propriety, but she was not crying.

'You see it's easier than you were expecting. For quite a time I've been afraid, and I was always imploring René to give those people up. He has a good job. We were quite happy. We were not rich, but we weren't doing badly. I don't know who he met . . .'

'How long ago?'

'About six months . . . It was last winter . . . Or rather, autumn . . . I'm just glad it's over, because now I needn't be so scared . . . You're sure that woman knows how to look after my little boy?'

'You needn't feel uneasy about that.'

'He's highly strung, like his father. He gets restless during the night . . .'

One could sense that she was tired, rather lost, trying to straighten out her thoughts.

'One thing I can tell you for certain is that René didn't shoot.'

'How do you know?'

'In the first place because he's incapable of it. He let himself be led astray by those people, never imagining things would get so serious.'

'Did he talk to you about it?'

'I'd noticed for some time that he was bringing home more money than he should. And he was going out more often, nearly always with Joseph Raison. Then, one day, I found his gun.'

'What did he say?'

'That I needn't worry, and that in a few months we should be able to go and live quietly in the South. He wanted to have a shop of his own, at Cannes or Nice . . .'

She was crying at last – softly, in little jerks.

'It's that car that's to blame, really . . . He'd set his heart on a Floride . . . He signed some bills . . . And the time came when he had to meet them . . . When he finds out I've told you, he'll be angry with me . . . Perhaps he won't want to have anything more to do with me . . .'

Sounds were heard from the corridor, and Maigret signed to Janvier to take the girl into the next room. He had recognized Buffet's voice.

There were three detectives, pushing in front of them a handcuffed man who threw Maigret a sharp, defiant glance.

'And the woman?' queried the superintendent.

'At the other end of the corridor. She's more dangerous than he is – she claws and bites.'

And indeed Buffet's face was scratched and there was blood on his nose.

'Come in, Fernand.'

Buffet came in as well, while his two officers remained outside. The ex-convict inspected his surroundings and re-marked:

'I rather think I've been here before.'

He was recovering his mocking, self-assured manner.

'I suppose you're going to plague the life out of me with questions like last time. I may as well warn you at once that I shan't answer them.'

'Who is your solicitor?'

'Still the same one. Maître Gambier.'

'Do you want us to send for him?'

'Personally, I've nothing to say to him. But if it amuses you to get the man out of bed . . .'

All through the night people were bustling to and fro in the corridors of the Quai des Orfèvres and going from office to office. Typewriters clicked like falling hailstones. The telephone rang uninterruptedly, for the public prosecutor's department was anxious to keep in touch and the examining magistrate had not gone to bed.

One of the inspectors spent most of his time making coffee. Now and then Maigret, as he went about the building, ran into one of his staff.

'Nothing yet?'

'He's not said a word.'

None of the three men from the Café des Amis would admit to recognizing Fernand. They were all playing the same game.

'Fernand – who's that?'

When the tape-recording of the call to Corbeil was played back to them, they replied:

'That's René's business. His love-affairs don't concern us.'

René himself retorted:

'I suppose I can have a mistress, can't I?'

Madame Lussac was confronted with Fernand.

'Do you recognize him?'

'No.'

'What did I tell you?' the ex-convict crowed jubilantly. 'None of these people have ever seen me before. When I left Saint-Martin-de-Ré I was flat broke, and a pal gave me his girl's address, saying she would see I didn't starve. I was in her house, lying low.'

Maître Gambier arrived at one o'clock in the morning and at once began to raise points of law.

According to the new Code of Criminal Procedure, the

police could only hold these men for twenty-four hours, after which the case would pass to the public prosecutor and the examining magistrate, who would have to take full responsibility for it.

Doubts could already be sensed among the Palais de Justice people.

A confrontation between Madame Lussac and her husband gave no results.

'Tell them the truth.'

'What do you mean, the truth? That I've got a mistress?'

'The revolver . . .'

'One of my buddies slipped me a gun. And so what? I do a lot of travelling, alone in my car . . .'

First thing in the morning they would round up the witnesses, all those who had already filed through the Quai des Orfèvres – the waiters from the café in the Rue La Fayette, the woman at the cash-desk, the beggar, the passers-by, and the police constable in mufti who had shot Raison.

Also first thing in the morning, they would search the flats of the three men arrested at the Porte de Versailles, and perhaps find the briefcase in one of them.

It had all boiled down to a matter of routine – rather sickening and burdensome routine.

'You can go back to Fontenay-aux-Roses now, but the welfare officer will stay with you for the time being . . .'

He told someone to drive her home. She was dropping with fatigue and stared round wide-eyed, as though wondering where she had got to.

While his man continued to press the prisoners with questions, Maigret went out for a breath of air and found that his hat and shoulders were white with the first snowflakes. A bar in the Boulevard du Palais was just opening; he went in and propped his elbows on the counter, eating hot croissants and drinking two or three cups of coffee.

He went back to the office at seven o'clock, trudging along and blinking his eyes, and was surprised to find Fumel there.

'Have you got hold of something, too?'

The inspector seemed highly excited, and began a voluble explanation.

'I was on duty last night. They told me what you were doing in the Avenue de Versailles, but it wasn't my show; so I took the chance to ring up friends in other parts of Paris. They all have Cuendet's photo.

'I said to myself that sooner or later it might lead to something . . .

'So I was chatting with Duffieux of the 18th *arrondissement*, and I mentioned my chap. And Duffieux said he'd been meaning to ring me on that subject.

'He works with your friend Inspector Lognon. When Lognon saw the photo, yesterday morning, he jumped, and put it in his pocket without a word.

'Cuendet's face reminded him of something. It seems he began asking questions in the bars and little restaurants in the Rue Caulaincourt and the Place Constantin-Pecqueur.

'As you know, when Lognon gets an idea into his head, he sticks to it. In the end he found what he was after – a place called the Régence, right at the top of the Rue Caulaincourt.

'They recognized Cuendet at once there, and told Lognon he used to come quite often, with a woman.'

'Had he been coming for long?' asked Maigret.

'Yes, that's what's so interesting. For years, according to them.'

'Do they know the woman?'

'The waiter doesn't know her by name, but he's positive she lives close by, because he sees her going past every morning, on her way to the shops.'

The entire staff of the Judicial Police was busy with Fernand and his gang. In another two hours the corridors would again be packed with witnesses, to each of whom the four men would be shown separately. It would take all day, and every typewriter in the building would be needed for copying statements.

Alone and unconcerned amid this bustle, Inspector Fumel, his fingers stained with nicotine from the cigarettes he always smoked to the very end – so that there was even an indelible mark on his lower lip – had come to talk to Maigret about the placid Swiss from Vaud, whom everyone else seemed to have forgotten.

The whole subject had apparently been dismissed. Cajou, the examining magistrate, felt sure he need give no more thought to it.

He had settled the question in his own mind the very first day:

*Vendetta in the underworld . . .*

Cajou didn't know old Justine, or the little flat in the Rue Mouffetard – let alone the Hôtel Lambert and the mansion it overlooked.

'Are you tired?'

'Not really.'

'Suppose we go up there together?'

Maigret spoke almost furtively, as though suggesting to Fumel that they should play truant from school.

'By the time we get there it will be daylight . . .'

He left instructions for his men, stopped to buy some tobacco at the corner shop by the river, and went off with Fumel – who was shivering with cold – to the Montmartre bus-stop.

# Chapter Seven

Did Lognon suspect that Maigret was more interested in the man killed in the Bois de Boulogne – and almost universally ignored – than in the Rue La Fayette hold-up and the gang that all the papers would be full of tomorrow morning?

If he did, wouldn't he have followed up the clue he had discovered? In that case one couldn't say how far he might not have gone towards finding out the truth – for he was perhaps the most intuitive member of the Paris police force – the most persistent, too, and the most desperately anxious for success.

Had he been dogged by bad luck, or did the fault lie in his conviction that fate was against him – that he was marked down in advance for victimization?

In any case he would end his career as an inspector at the police station in the 18th *arrondissement*, just like Aristide Fumel in the 16th. Fumel's wife had gone away and left him; Lognon's was an invalid who had not stopped complaining for the last fifteen years.

The Cuendet business had probably been sheer accident. Lognon, busy with some other matter, had mentioned his discovery to a colleague – who had seen no great importance in it, for he had spoken of it quite casually when Fumel rang him up.

The snow was falling fairly hard now, and beginning to settle on the roofs; not in the street, unfortunately. Maigret always felt disappointed to see it melting on the pavement.

The bus was stiflingly hot. Most of the passengers sat

silently, looking straight ahead of them, their heads lolling from side to side, their faces blank.

'No news of the rug?'

Fumel jumped. His thoughts had been far away.

'The rug?' he repeated, as though he had not understood.

'The wild-cat fur rug.'

'I looked into Stuart Wilton's car, but I didn't see any rug. The car not only has a heater, it's air-conditioned as well. It even has a little bar – so I was told by one of the garage men.'

'What about the son's car?'

'He usually parks it outside the George V. I took a quick glance at it, but I saw no rug there, either.'

'D'you know where he gets his petrol?'

'Usually from a pump in the Rue Marbeuf.'

'Been round there?'

'I've not had time yet.'

The bus stopped at the corner of the Place Constantin-Pecqueur. There was hardly anyone about. It was not yet eight o'clock.

'This must be the place.'

The lights were on, and a waiter was sweeping up the saw-dust on the floor. It was one of the old-fashioned brasseries that are becoming very rare in Paris, with metal globes to hold dusters, a marble-topped bar where a woman would arrive later to sit behind the till, and mirrors all round the walls. Notices hung here and there, recommending the *choucroute garnie* and the *cassoulet*.

The two men went in.

'Had any breakfast?'

'Not yet.'

Fumel ordered coffee and brioches, while Maigret – who had drunk too much coffee during the night and whose mouth felt clammy with it – asked for a small brandy.

Outside, it seemed difficult for life to start up again. It was neither night nor day. Children were going past on their way to school, trying to catch the falling snowflakes in their mouths, though the snow must have a dusty taste.

'Tell me, waiter . . .'

'Yes, sir?'

'Do you recognize this man?'

The waiter looked knowingly at the superintendent.

'You're Monsieur Maigret, aren't you? I recognize you. You came here a couple of years ago with Inspector Lognon.'

He gave a benevolent glance at the photograph.

'Yes, he's a regular customer. He always comes with the little lady with the hats.'

'Why do you call her the little lady with the hats?'

'Because she has a different hat nearly every time – smart, amusing ones. They usually come for dinner and sit at the back, in that corner. They're a nice couple. She has a passion for *choucroute*. They take their time, and end up with coffee and liqueurs, sitting hand in hand.'

'Have they been coming here for long?'

'For years. I don't know how many.'

'It seems she lives in this district?'

'I've been asked that before. She must have a flat somewhere round here, because I see her going past every morning with her shopping-bag.'

Maigret was delighted, without knowing why, to discover that there had been a woman in Honoré Cuendet's life.

A little later he and Fumel walked into the concierge's lodge of the first house they came to; the morning's letters were being sorted.

'Do you know this man?'

The concierge looked closely at the photograph and shook her head.

'I think I've seen him before, but I can't say I know him. In any case he's never been to this house.'

'You don't happen to have among your tenants a woman who often changes her hats?'

She stared at Maigret in bewilderment and shrugged her shoulders, muttering something he couldn't catch.

They had no better luck with the second and third houses. At the fourth, they found the concierge bandaging her husband's hand; he had cut himself while putting out the dustbins.

'Do you know him?'

'And what if I do?'

'Does he live here?'

'He does and he doesn't. He's the gentleman friend of the little lady on the fifth floor.'

'What little lady?'

'Mademoiselle Eveline, who makes hats.'

'Has she been long in the house?'

'At least twelve years. She was here before I came.'

'Was he with her already?'

'Maybe he was. I don't remember.'

'Have you seen them lately?'

'I see her every day, of course.'

'And him?'

'D'you remember when he was here last, Désiré?' she asked her husband.

'No, but it's quite a time.'

'Did he ever stay the night?'

She seemed to find the superintendent childish.

'What if he did? They're of age, aren't they?'

'He used to stay here for several days?'

'Even for weeks.'

'Is Mademoiselle Eveline at home? What is her surname?'

'Schneider.'

'Does she get many letters?'

The bundle of unsorted letters still lay on the ledge in front of the pigeon-holes.

'Practically none.'

'The fifth floor – on the left?'

'No – the right.'

Maigret went out into the street to see if there was any light showing from the flat. There was, so he began to climb the stairs with Fumel. The house had no lift. The staircase was tidy, the house clean and quiet, with mats outside the doors and here and there a brass or enamel plate.

They noticed a dentist on the second floor, a midwife on the third. Maigret halted now and then to recover his breath, and heard sounds of a wireless.

Reaching the fifth floor, he felt almost reluctant to ring the bell. Here, too, the radio had been playing; but now it was switched off and steps were heard approaching. The door opened, and a small, slim, fair-haired woman, garbed not in a dressing-gown but in a kind of overall, and holding a dish-cloth, stood looking at them with wide blue eyes.

Maigret and Fumel felt no less embarrassed than she, as they watched her expression of astonishment give way to one of alarm. Her lip quivered as she murmured at last:

'Are you bringing me bad news?'

She beckoned them into the living-room she had just been tidying, and pushed aside the vacuum cleaner that stood in the way.

'Why do you ask me that?'

'I don't know . . . Visitors, at this hour of the morning, and when Honoré's been away so long . . .'

She must be about forty-five, but she still looked very youthful. Her skin was clear and her figure firm and rounded.

'Are you from the police?'

'I am Superintendent Maigret. And this is Inspector Fumel.'

'Has Honoré had an accident?'

'You were right in guessing I had bad news for you.'

She was not crying yet, and they felt she was clinging for support to commonplace phrases.

'Please sit down. Do take off your overcoat, it's very hot in here. Honoré likes warmth. You mustn't mind the untidiness . . .'

'You're very fond of him?'

She bit her lip, trying to guess how serious the news might be.

'He's had an accident?'

Then, almost at once:

'He's dead?'

Now she began to cry – like a child, with her mouth open, not caring whether she looked ugly. She grasped her hair with both hands and stared round as though looking for a corner where she could hide.

'I always had a foreboding . . .'

'Why?'

'I don't know . . . We were too happy . . .'

The room was comfortable, cosy, the furniture heavy but good, and the few ornaments not in the worst of taste. An open door led into a cheerful kitchen, with a place still laid for breakfast.

'Please don't take any notice . . .' she kept saying, 'Excuse me . . .'

She opened another door, into the bedroom which was still in darkness; went in, and threw herself face downwards across the bed, crying her heart out.

Maigret and Fumel exchanged glances in silence, and the inspector was the more moved of the two; he always had a soft spot for women, in spite of all the trouble they had brought him.

It didn't last as long as one might have feared; then she went into the bathroom, splashed her face with cold water, and came back looking almost composed.

'I must apologize,' she said quietly. 'How did it happen?'

'He was found dead in the Bois de Boulogne. Haven't you seen the newspapers these last few days?'

'I never read newspapers. But why the Bois de Boulogne? What can he have been doing there?'

'He had been murdered in some other place.'

'Murdered? But why?'

She was trying hard not to burst into tears again.

'You had been friends for a long time?'

'More than ten years.'

'Where did you first meet him?'

'In a restaurant just near here.'

'The Régence?'

'Yes. I used to go there now and then for a meal. I noticed him, alone in his corner.'

Did this mean that about that time Cuendet had been planning a burglary in the district? Very likely. A scrutiny of the list of unsolved burglaries would no doubt reveal one committed in the Rue Caulaincourt.

'I don't remember how we first got into conversation. But one evening we had dinner at the same table. He asked if I were German and I told him Alsatian. I was born at Strasbourg.'

She smiled wanly.

'We used to make fun of each other's accents – he still had his Swiss one and I'd never lost my Alsatian one.'

Hers was a pleasant, sing-song accent. Madame Maigret, too, was from Alsace, and of much the same height and figure.

'He became your lover?'

She blew her nose: it was red, but she didn't care.

'He wasn't always here. He hardly ever spent more than two or three weeks with me, then he'd go off on a trip. At first I used to wonder if he hadn't got a wife and family in the provinces. Some men keep quiet about that when they come up to Paris . . .'

This suggested that there had been other men in her life before Cuendet.

'How did you find out he wasn't like that?'

'He wasn't married, was he?'

'No.'

'I felt sure he wasn't. For one thing, I guessed he had no children of his own, from the way he looked at other people's in the street. One felt he was resigned to not being a father, but that he regretted it all the same. And when he came here he didn't behave like a married man. It's hard to explain. He had a kind of bashfulness that a married man would have lost. The first time, for instance, I realized he felt shy about being in my bed, and when he woke up next morning he was even more embarrassed . . .'

'He never talked to you about his occupation?'

'No.'

'And you never asked him?'

'I tried to find out without seeming to pry . . .'

'He told you he travelled a lot?'

'He said he had to go away. He never explained where, or why. One day I asked him if his mother was still living, and he blushed. That gave me the idea that perhaps he lived with her. Anyway he had someone to mend his clothes and darn his socks – someone who didn't do it very well. Buttons were always coming loose, for instance; I used to tease him about it.'

'When did he leave you for the last time?'

'Six weeks ago. I can look up the exact date . . .'

It was her turn to ask a question:

'And when . . . when did it happen?'

'On Friday.'

'And yet he never had much money on him.'

'When he came to stay with you, did he bring a suitcase?'

'No. If you look in the wardrobe you'll find his dressing-gown and slippers, and there are shirts, socks and pyjamas in a drawer.'

She pointed to the mantelpiece and Maigret saw three pipes there, one of them a meerschaum . . . Here too, just as in the Rue Mouffetard, there was a stove with an armchair beside it – Honoré Cuendet's armchair.

'I am sorry to be indiscreet, but there is a question I must ask you.'

'I can guess what it is. You mean, about money?'

'Yes. Used he to give you any?'

'He suggested it, but I refused, because I make quite a good living. I did allow him to pay half the rent – he insisted, and it made him uncomfortable to live here without paying his share.

'He used to give me presents. He bought the furniture for this room, and had my trying-on room done up. I'll show it to you . . .'

It was a very small room, furnished in the Louis XVI style, with a profusion of mirrors.

'He painted all the walls too, including the kitchen, and papered the living-room. He loved doing odd jobs.'

'How did he spend his days?'

'He went out for walks – not long ones, just round here, always the same way, like somebody taking out a dog. And he sat in his chair, reading. You'll find heaps of books in the cupboard, nearly all of them travel books.'

'You never went away with him?'

'We had a few days at Dieppe the second year. Another time we went on holiday to Savoy and he showed me the Swiss mountains in the distance and told me that was his country. And another time we took a coach trip to Nice and along the Riviera.'

'He spent money lavishly?'

'It depends what you mean by lavish. He wasn't stingy, but

he didn't like to be cheated, and he always looked over our hotel and restaurant bills.'

'I take it your age is about forty?'

'Forty-four.'

'So you have some experience of the world. Did you never wonder why he was leading this double life? Or why he didn't marry you?'

'I've known other men who didn't propose marriage.'

'But were they his type?'

'No, of course they weren't.'

She pondered for a moment.

'I did wonder about things, naturally. At first, as I told you, I thought he must have a wife in the provinces and a job that brought him to Paris several times a year. I shouldn't have blamed him. It would be tempting to have a woman to welcome him here, and a home to go to. He loathed hotels, I noticed that the first time we went away together. He felt uncomfortable in a hotel. As though he were afraid of something all the time.'

(Only natural!)

'Later, from the way he behaved and the way his socks were darned, I decided he must live with his mother and that he didn't like to tell me about it. There are more men than you'd suppose who don't marry because of their mothers, and are as much in awe of them at fifty years old as when they were little boys. It might have been that way with him.'

'All the same, he had to earn his living.'

'He might have had a small business somewhere.'

'You never suspected another kind of activity?'

'What kind?'

She was perfectly sincere; there was no question of her acting the innocent.

'What do you mean? I'm ready for anything now. What did he do?'

'He was a thief, Mademoiselle Schneider.'

'He – Honoré?'

She gave a nervous giggle.

'You don't really mean that, do you?'

'Wait a moment! He had been a thief all his life, from the age of sixteen, when he was apprenticed to a locksmith at Lausanne. He ran away from an approved school in Switzerland and joined the Foreign Legion.'

'He said something about the Legion when I noticed his tattoo-marks.'

'He didn't mention that he'd spent two years in prison?'

Her knees gave way and she sat down abruptly, and listened as though the Cuendet she was hearing about were a different man from her Honoré.

Now and then she shook her head, still incredulous.

'I arrested him myself on that first occasion, mademoiselle, and since then he had been brought to my office several times. He was no ordinary thief. He had no accomplices, never associated with criminals, and led a very regular life. From time to time he would get an idea for a burglary by reading the newspapers and magazines, and for weeks he would watch a particular house, with all its comings and goings . . .

'Until the moment when he felt confident enough to go in and pick up the jewels and money he found there.'

'I simply can't believe it! It's too incredible!'

'I can quite understand you. But you were right about his mother. For part of the time he didn't spend here he used to be with her, in a flat in the Rue Mouffetard where he also kept belongings.'

'Does she know?'

'Yes.'

'She's known all along?'

'Yes.'

'And she didn't try to stop him?'

She was not indignant, only astonished.

'Is that why he was killed?'

'More than likely.'

'The police?'

She stiffened, her expression became less friendly, less trustful.

'No.'

'Was it the people where . . . whose house he had burgled, who killed him?'

'I imagine so. Now listen to me. I am not in charge of the investigation; it is in the hands of Monsieur Cajou, the examining magistrate. He has given certain tasks to Inspector Fumel.'

Fumel bowed.

'This morning the inspector is here unofficially, without instructions. You would have been entitled to refuse to answer our questions. You could have refused to let us in. And if we were to search your flat, we would be exceeding our authority. You understand?'

No. Maigret perceived that she did not grasp the implications of what he had been saying.

'I think . . .'

'To put it more precisely, nothing you have told us about Cuendet will appear in the inspector's report. It is to be expected that when he finds out about your existence and your relations with Honoré, the examining magistrate will send Fumel or another inspector to call on you, with a proper warrant.'

'What should I do then?'

'When that happens, you will be entitled to ask for your lawyer to be present.'

'Why?'

'I said you would be entitled to. The law does not insist on your doing so. Perhaps Cuendet may have left something in your flat, in addition to his clothes, his books and his pipes . . .'

At last he saw understanding dawn in Mademoiselle Schneider's blue eyes. Too late, for already she was murmuring, as if to herself:

'The suitcase . . .'

'It would be only natural for Honoré, since he spent part of the year under your roof, to have left in your care a suitcase containing personal effects. It would also be only natural for him to have given you the key, telling you – for instance – to open it if anything should happen to him . . .'

Maigret rather wished Fumel were not present; and as though aware of this, the inspector had put on a glum, absent-minded expression.

As for Eveline, she shook her head.

'I haven't got the key . . . But . . .'

'That doesn't matter, either. It is quite on the cards that a man like Cuendet would have taken the precaution of making a will, instructing you to see to various things in the event of his death – if only to take care of his mother . . .'

'Is she very old?'

'You will be seeing her yourself, since it appears that you two were the only women in his life.'

'You believe so?'

She could not help being pleased, and showing it by her smile. When she smiled she had dimples, like quite a young girl.

'I don't know what to think, myself.'

'When we've gone you will have time to think things over at leisure.'

'Tell me, superintendent . . .'

She paused, suddenly blushing to the roots of her hair.

'He never . . . he never killed anyone?'

'Never – I can assure you.'

'You know, if you'd told me he had, I shouldn't have believed you.'

'I'll tell you something else, more difficult to explain. Cuendet lived on part of what he got by theft, that's certain . . .'

'He spent so little!'

'Precisely. It is possible, even probable, that he felt a need for security, a need to know that he had a nest-egg to fall back on. But I wouldn't be surprised if in his particular case there was another essential factor.

'As I told you, he used to study the life of a house for weeks on end . . .'

'How did he set about it?'

'By choosing a convenient bistro where he would sit for hours in the window; or when he had the opportunity, by renting a room in the house opposite.'

Eveline was struck by the same idea that had occurred to Maigret.

'Do you suppose that when I first met him, at the Régence . . . ?'

'Very likely. He didn't wait for a flat to be empty, for the owners to go out. On the contrary, he used to wait till they got home . . .'

'Why?'

'A psychologist or a psychiatrist could answer that question better than I can. Was the sense of danger necessary to him? I'm not so sure. You see, he didn't only break into a strange flat, but into the lives of the people who lived there, so to speak. They'd be asleep in their beds, and he brushed past them. It was rather as though, as well as their jewellery, he carried off a little of their private lives . . .'

'You don't seem to have any feeling against him . . .'

It was Maigret's turn to smile at this, but he only growled:

'I have no feeling against anybody. Goodbye, mademoiselle. Don't forget what I said to you, not a single word of it. Think it over quietly.'

He shook hands with her, to her great surprise, and Fumel did the same, more awkwardly, as though in the grip of emotion.

They were no sooner on the stairs than Fumel exclaimed:
'That's a wonderful woman!'

He would be back again, hanging round the neighbourhood, even after everyone had forgotten Honoré Cuendet. He couldn't help himself. He was already saddled with a mistress who gave him endless trouble, and he would now be doing his best to complicate his life still further.

Outside, the snow was beginning to settle on the pavements.

'What do I do now, chief?'

'You must be sleepy – no? Anyhow, let's have a drink.'

By this time there were a few customers at the Régence; one of them, a commercial traveller, was copying addresses from the trade directory.

'Did you find her?' asked the waiter.

'Yes.'

'Nice isn't she? What will you have?'

'A hot grog for me.'

'The same for me.'

'Two grogs, two!'

'This afternoon, when you've had some sleep, you'll be writing your report.'

'I'm to put in about the Rue Neuve Saint-Pierre?'

'Yes, of course, and about the Wilton woman who lives opposite the Hôtel Lambert. Cajou will send for you to ask for details.'

'He'll tell me to go and search Mademoiselle Schneider's flat.'

'Where, I hope, you will find nothing except a suitcase full of clothes.'

In spite of his admiration for the superintendent, Fumel felt uneasy, and puffed nervously at his cigarette.

'I understood what you were saying to her.'

'Honoré's mother told me, "I'm sure my son won't leave me without a penny."'

'She said the same to me.'

'You'll see, Cajou won't be at all keen for this case to go any further. As soon as he hears the name of Wilton . . .'

Maigret sipped his grog slowly, paid for the drinks, and decided to take a taxi back to the office.

'Can I drop you anywhere?'

'No, I have a direct bus.'

Perhaps, fearing that Eveline had not quite understood, Fumel intended to go back for a word with her.

'By the way, I'm bothered about that matter of the rug. So keep on looking into that . . .'

And thrusting his hands into his pockets, Maigret walked off to the taxi rank in the Place Constantin-Pecqueur, from where he could see the windows of Inspector Lognon's flat.

# Chapter Eight

At the Quai des Orfèvres everyone was worn out – the inspectors, as well as the men who had been arrested during the night. The witnesses had been fetched from their homes and they were all over the place, some of them half-asleep and very peevish, plaguing Joseph, the office messenger, with questions:

'How much longer will they keep us hanging about?'

What could the old man tell them? He knew no more about it than they did.

The waiter from the Brasserie Dauphine was arriving with yet another tray of rolls and coffee.

The first thing Maigret did on getting back to his office was to ring through to Moers, who was equally busy upstairs, in the Judicial Identity service.

The 'paraffin test' had been applied to the four men's hands, so that if any of them had used a firearm of any kind within the past three or four days, gunpowder would be found in the pores of his skin, even if he had taken the precaution of wearing gloves

'Have you got the results?'

'They've just come from the laboratory.'

'Which of the four?'

'Number three.'

Maigret glanced down the list, which bore a number against each name. Number three was Roger Stieb, a Czechoslovak refugee who had worked for a long time in the same factory as Joseph Raison, on the Quai de Javel.

'The expert is quite positive?'

'Absolutely.'

'Nothing from the other three?'

'Nothing.'

Stieb was a tall, fair-haired youth who had been the most docile of the lot during the night's questioning. Torrence was still pressing him hard, but he merely gazed at the inspector with bovine placidity, as though he did not understand a word of French.

All the same, he was the gang's killer, responsible for covering their escape after an attack.

The other man, Loubières, was a burly, hirsute fellow, born at Fécamp, who now kept a garage at Puteaux. He was married, with two children. A team of experts was searching his premises at the moment.

Nothing had been found at René Lussac's flat, or in Rosalie's villa.

Rosalie herself had been the noisiest of the lot, and Maigret could hear her yapping, although the office where she was having her *tête-à-tête* with Lucas was two doors farther down the passage.

Some of the witnesses were now being confronted with the prisoners. The two waiters were too scared to speak positively, but said they thought they recognized Fernand as the customer who had been in the café at the time of the hold-up.

'You're sure you've caught the whole bunch?' they had asked before the identification began.

They were told that was so, although it was not strictly true. One member of the gang – the driver of the car – was still at large and the police had no clues to his identity.

He must be a crack driver, as always in such cases, but probably he played no part in the actual operations.

Maigret had to take a call from the public prosecutor.

'Yes, sir ... We're getting on ... We know who did the shooting – it was Stieb ... Yes, he denies it ... He'll deny it to the bitter end ... they all will.'

Except poor Madame Lussac, who was in a state of collapse at home, where the woman welfare officer was helping her to look after her baby.

Maigret could hardly keep his eyes open, and the hot grog he had drunk at the Régence was no help. He was reduced to fetching the bottle of brandy he kept in his cupboard for special occasions, and taking a reluctant nip from that.

'Hello? Not yet, sir.' This time it was the examining magistrate.

Maigret kept getting calls on two telephones simultaneously, and not till twenty-past ten did the one he wanted come through – from Puteaux.

'We've found it, chief.'

'The lot?'

'Down to the last note.'

The newspapers had been allowed to announce that the bank had the numbers of the stolen notes. This was not true, but it had prevented the thieves from trying to get rid of them. They had been waiting for a chance to unload them in the provinces or abroad. Fernand was cunning enough to bide his time and to stop his men from leaving Paris while the search was in full cry.

'Where?'

'In the coachwork of an old car. That Loubières woman is the bossy type, she stuck to us like a leech ...'

'You think she was in the know?'

'I do. We searched the cars one by one. More or less took 'em to pieces, in fact. Anyhow – we've got the stuff!'

'Don't forget to make Madame Loubières sign the statement.'

'She won't. I've tried.'

'Then get some witnesses.'

'That's what I've done.'

For Maigret this practically settled the matter. He would not be needed while the witnesses were being questioned, separately and in pairs. That would take hours.

Afterwards, the inspectors would make their individual reports to him, and he would have to draw up a general report.

'Would you get me Monsieur Dupont d'Hastier, the public prosecutor?'

A moment later he announced:

'The notes have been found.'

'And the briefcase?'

The man expected too much. Why not ask for nice, clear fingerprints?

'The briefcase is floating down the Seine by now, unless it was burnt in someone's stove.'

'Where was the money found?'

'At the garage.'

'What does the garage-owner say?'

'Nothing, so far. He hasn't been told about it.'

'Take care to have his solicitor there. I don't want any complaints, or any trouble in court when the case comes up for hearing.'

Once the corridors were cleared the two men would be taken to the Central Police Station, and the woman Rosalie, too – she would be put in a room by herself – and there would be made to strip to the skin and go through the anthropometrical inspection. At least two of them had had that experience before.

They would probably spend the night in a ground-floor cell, because the examining magistrate would want to see them in the morning before committing them to the Santé prison.

It would be several months before the case came up for trial, and other gangs would have had time to form by then, in the same way, for reasons with which the superintendent was not concerned.

He opened one door, then another, and found Lucas sitting in front of a typewriter, typing with two fingers, while Rosalie paced to and fro with her hands on her hips.

'So there you are! Pleased with yourself, I suppose? The idea of Fernand being out of clink was keeping you awake at night, till you found an excuse for getting your paws on him again. You're not even ashamed to torment a woman; you forget that in the old days you sometimes came to my bar for a drink, and you weren't above picking up the bits of information I could give you . . .'

She was the only one who was not sleepy, whose energy showed no sign of flagging.

'And on purpose to humiliate me, you turn me over to the smallest of all your inspectors. A fellow I could swallow at one gulp!'

Maigret made no reply, merely saying to Lucas, with a wink:

'I'm going home for a couple of hours' sleep. The money's been found.'

'What's that?' screeched the woman.

'Don't leave her alone. Send for whoever you like to keep her company – a tall chap if she'd rather – and go and sit in my office.'

'Right, chief.'

He had himself driven home in a police car. The courtyard was full of them, for all resources had been mobilized since the previous evening.

'I hope you're going to bed?' said his wife as she turned down the sheet. 'What time shall I call you?'

'At half-past twelve.'

'As early as that?'

He hadn't the energy to take a bath at once. He would have one when he woke up. He was just dozing off, warm to the ears, when the telephone rang.

He reached out for it and growled:

'Maigret speaking – yes?'

'Fumel here, superintendent . . .'

'I'm sorry. I was half-asleep. Where are you?'

'Rue Marbeuf.'

'Go ahead.'

'I have some news. About the rug.'

'You've found it?'

'No. I doubt if it will ever be found. But it did exist. The man at the petrol pump in the Rue Marbeuf is positive. He noticed it again about a week ago.'

'Why did he notice it?'

'Because it's unusual to see a rug in a smart sports car – especially a fur rug.'

'When did he see it last?'

'He's not certain, but he says it was quite recently. But two or three days ago, when young Wilton called in for petrol, it had gone.'

'Put that in your report.'

'What will happen, in your opinion?'

Maigret, eager to bring the conversation to an end, replied laconically:

'Nothing!' and hung up. He needed sleep. And he felt almost certain he was right.

Nothing would happen!

He could imagine how supercilious the examining magistrate would look if he, Maigret, went and told him:

'On the night of Friday to Saturday, about one o'clock, Honoré Cuendet broke into the private house belonging to Florence Wilton, née Lenoir, in the Rue Neuve Saint-Pierre.'

'How do you know?'

'Because for the last five weeks he had been studying the house, from a room in the Hôtel Lambert.'

'So, just because a man takes a room in a shady hotel, you jump to the conclusion . . .'

'This was no ordinary man, it was Honoré Cuendet, who for nearly thirty years . . .'

He would describe Cuendet's ways.

'Have you ever caught him red-handed?'

Maigret would be compelled to admit that he hadn't.

'He had keys to the house?'

'No.'

'Accomplices inside it?'

'That is unlikely.'

'And Mrs Wilton and the servants were there at the time?'

'Cuendet never broke into unoccupied houses.'

'You are suggesting that this woman . . .'

'Not her. Her lover.'

'How do you know she has a lover?'

'I was told by a prostitute named Olga, who also lives opposite.'

'Has she seen them in bed together?'

'She's seen the man's car.'

'And who is this lover?'

'Young Wilton.'

Here the picture became a little blurred, because Maigret saw the examining magistrate laugh derisively, which was out of character.

'You are insinuating that this woman and her stepson . . .'

'Well, the father and his daughter-in-law didn't hesitate . . .'

'What is that?'

Maigret would relate the story of Lida, who had been the father's mistress after marrying the son.

Come, come! As though such things were possible! How could a conscientious magistrate, belonging to one of the best professional families in Paris, contemplate for a single moment . . .

'I hope you have further evidence?'

'Yes, sir . . .'

He must be asleep, for he saw himself bringing out of his pocket a twist of tissue-paper containing two almost invisible threads.

'What is this?'

'These are hairs, sir.'

Another proof that this was a dream, that it could only be a dream: now the magistrate was saying:

'Whose hairs?'

'They come from a wild-cat.'

'Why wild?'

'Because the rug in the car was made of wild-cat fur. For once in his long career, Cuendet must have made a noise, knocked something over, given the alarm, and they bashed him over the head.

'The lovers couldn't call the police without . . .'

Without what? His ideas were growing slightly confused. Without Stuart Wilton finding out what was going on, of course. And Stuart Wilton held the purse-strings . . .

Neither Florence nor her lover knew the unknown man who had suddenly appeared in their room. Wasn't it a wise precaution to make his face unrecognizable?

He had bled profusely, so they had been obliged to clean up . . .

And then the car . . .

And there, he had messed up the rug . . .

'You understand, sir . . .'

There he would be, apologetically, with his two hairs.

'In the first place, who told you these were wild-cat hairs?'

'An expert.'

'And another expert will come into the witness-box to jeer

at him and declare they are hairs of some completely different animal . . .'

The magistrate was right. That was how it would happen. There would be a burst of laughter in court, and Counsel for the Defence would raise his hands dramatically and protest:

'Now gentlemen, please let us be serious . . . What is the evidence against my client? Two hairs . . .'

Things might, of course, be done differently. For instance, Maigret might pay a call on Florence Wilton, put questions to her, poke about the house, question the servants.

And in the quiet of his own office, he might have a long talk with young Wilton.

But that sort of thing was against regulations.

'That will be enough, Maigret. Forget all this far-fetched stuff and take away those hairs . . .'

In any case he didn't give a damn. That was why he had winked at Fumel this morning.

Would the inspector, so unhappy in love, be more successful with Eveline than he'd been with other women?

At all events, the old lady in the Rue Mouffetard had been right.

'*I know my son . . . I'm sure he won't leave me without a penny . . .*'

How much money was there in the . . . ?

Maigret was sound asleep.

No one would ever know.

*Noland*
*23 January 1961*

# PENGUIN RED CLASSICS

**THE MAN ON THE BOULEVARD**
GEORGES SIMENON

'Simenon's Maigret, cool and classic as ever … All mystery buffs should celebrate' Scott Turow

Louis Thouret is found stabbed in an alleyway off the Boulevard Saint-Martin in Paris. His wife seems strangely calm when she identifies the body and is more surprised to see that he is wearing clothes she has never seen before.

As Chief Superintendent Maigret pieces together the dead man's last days, he discovers that Louis had a secret life. He left his job years ago. Somehow he had enough money to convince his conventional wife he was still working. But who would want to kill him? Especially when it seems he just spent his days sitting on a bench on the boulevard, watching the world go by …

**For more classic fiction, read Red**
**www.penguinclassics.com/reds**

# PENGUIN RED CLASSICS

**THE FRIEND OF MADAME MAIGRET**
GEORGES SIMENON

'A great novelist ... the sheer range of his understanding of the human heart is unparalleled in twentieth-century fiction' Paul Bailey

Maigret becomes increasingly frustrated as his attempts to prove that a brutal, repulsive murder has been committed at a local bookbinder prove fruitless. The mystery revolves around a series of seemingly unconnected incidents and characters, creating an intricate and complicated narrative set amongst the backdrop of the Marais district of Paris.

Eventually it is the intelligent and compassionate Madame Maigret who provides the vital clue ...

**For more classic fiction, read Red**

**www.penguinclassics.com/reds**

# PENGUIN RED CLASSICS

**A MAN'S HEAD**
GEORGES SIMENON

'Excellent … grips from the first line' *Independent*

A rich American widow and her maid have been stabbed to death in a brutal attack. All the evidence points to Joseph, a young drifter, and he is soon arrested. But what is his motive? Or is he just a pawn in a wider conspiracy?

Inspector Maigret believes the police have the wrong man and lets him escape from prison to prove his innocence. Perhaps, with Joseph on the loose, the real murderer will surface.

A deadly game of cross and double-cross has begun …

'A giant, a genius, a glorious storyteller' *Daily Telegraph*

**For more classic fiction, read Red**

**www.penguinclassics.com/reds**

# PENGUIN RED CLASSICS

**THE STRANGERS IN THE HOUSE**
GEORGES SIMENON

'A master storyteller … Simenon gave to the puzzle story a humanity
that it had never had before' *Daily Telegraph*

Hector Loursat, a lawyer in the town of Moulins, has lived as a
drunken recluse since his wife left him eighteen years before.
Estranged from society and even his own daughter, he shuts himself in
his study, numbed by endless bottles of burgundy. But when a dead
man is found in his flat one night, the resulting police investigation
unearths secrets that shake the town – and Loursat's seclusion – to the
core. No longer able to ignore the outside world, he begins to feel new
life running in his veins and emerges to take on the murder case
himself.

In the progressive breakdown of Loursat's self-imposed isolation,
Simenon brilliantly depicts the psychology of loneliness and a man's
tortured re-engagement with humanity and its darkest acts.

**For more classic fiction, read Red**

**www.penguinclassics.com/reds**

# PENGUIN RED CLASSICS

**MAIGRET IN COURT**
GEORGES SIMENON

'A unique teller of tales … What interested Simenon was the average man losing control of his own fate' *Observer*

Dreaming of his retirement to the Loire, Chief Inspector Maigret is dismayed to find himself once again embroiled in a brutal murder case. Gaston Meurant faces the Assizes Court on the charge of killing a small child, but, although the evidence points to his guilt, Maigret doubts that the mild-mannered picture framer can have committed such a horrific crime.

In the tense courtroom drama that ensues, Maigret must expose some unsavoury evidence about the accused man's private life in order to establish the truth and save him from execution, and sees the gentle Meurant turn into an obsessive and vengeful man in a search for justice outside the legal system.

**For more classic fiction, read Red**

**www.penguinclassics.com/reds**

# PENGUIN RED CLASSICS

**MAIGRET AND THE GHOST**
GEORGES SIMENON

'A novelist who entered his fictional world as if he were part of it'
Peter Ackroyd

Inspector Lognon – a plain-clothes detective with a reputation for
misfortune – is shot in the street with the word 'ghost' on his lips. It
soon emerges that he spent the night in the nearby apartment of a
beautiful young woman, who has since then vanished. While the
injured man fights for his life in hospital, Chief Superintendent Maigret
discovers that the hapless Inspector may finally have been on to
something big. And when he encounters suave art dealer Norris Jonker
and his glamorous wife Mirella, Maigret begins to wonder if their
strange lifestyle is the reason for Lognon's presence on the Avenue
Junot.

In *Maigret and the Ghost*, Simenon's tenacious detective is perplexed
by a constant stream of conflicting evidence as he explores the
underground world of art collecting.

**For more classic fiction, read Red**

**www.penguinclassics.com/reds**

# PENGUIN RED CLASSICS

**LOCK 14**
GEORGES SIMENON

'[Simenon's] peculiar accuracy of vision ... conveys with such a sure touch, the bleakness of human life' A. N. Wilson

One rainy night a canal worker stumbles across the strangled body of Mary Lampson in a stable near Lock 14. The dead woman's husband seems unmoved by her death and is curt and unhelpful when Maigret interviews him aboard his yacht. But gradually Maigret is able to piece together their story – a sordid tale of whisky-filled orgies and nomadic life on the canals. Can the answer to this crime be found aboard the yacht? Or is the murderer among the barges, carters and lock-keepers who work the canal?

In *Lock 14*, Simenon plunges Maigret into the unfamiliar canal world of shabby bars and shadowy towpaths, drawing together the strands of a tragic case of lost identity.

**For more classic fiction, read Red**

**www.penguinclassics.com/reds**